"You're assuming that [...] wish for a divorce," said Nicholas.

"You can't wish to stay married to someone who—who won't live with you." Cally said, slowly and unsteadily.

"Of course not." He sounded almost brisk. "Naturally I want a wife who'll share my home and my bed."

He smiled at her, his eyes touching her— stripping her, she realized, as her heart began to flutter in panic.

"In fact, I want you, my sweet," he added softly. "Because you stood beside me in church and made certain vows. I remember it perfectly. You were wearing a white dress with a lot of little buttons down the front of it. Frankly, I was fantasizing about undoing them all—with my teeth," he added, with a kind of sensuous reminiscence that made her shiver.

"Now, at last, I want those vows fulfilled, and I really think, my sweet, that I've waited long enough. Even you must agree that our wedding night is long overdue...."

Legally wed,
but he's never said...
"I love you."

They're...

The series where marriages are
made in haste...and love comes later....

Look out for more WEDLOCKED! wedding
stories available only from Harlequin Presents®

Look out for the next book in this miniseries:
The Antonides Marriage Deal
by Anne McAllister
#2533
April 2006

Sara Craven
HIS WEDDING-NIGHT HEIR

Wedlocked!

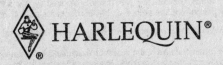

HARLEQUIN®

TORONTO • NEW YORK • LONDON
AMSTERDAM • PARIS • SYDNEY • HAMBURG
STOCKHOLM • ATHENS • TOKYO • MILAN • MADRID
PRAGUE • WARSAW • BUDAPEST • AUCKLAND

ISBN 0-373-12509-7

HIS WEDDING-NIGHT HEIR

First North American Publication 2005.

www.eHarlequin.com

Printed in U.S.A.

CHAPTER ONE

SHE was running. Forcing herself onwards down a long straight road, where flanking trees threw grotesque shadows in front of her. Shadows that she did not want to enter. Her breath tore at her lungs, and her legs ached, but she could not stop. And dared not look behind.

Must keep going. Need to move on. The words beat a rhythm in her brain. Have to run. Have to...

Cally Maitland sat up, gasping, her body damp with perspiration, as the sudden shrill of the alarm clock invaded her subconscious and brought her with shocking suddenness to the reality of a new day. She reached out a shaking hand and silenced the noise, then sank back against her pillow, trying to clear her head.

My God, she thought. What was all that about?

But of course she already knew. Because she'd had that dream before. Several times.

The sun was pouring into the room through a gap in the shabby curtains, and it was clearly a beautiful May day. But Cally felt a chill in the air, and wrapped her arms round her body with a faint shiver.

She said softly, half under her breath, 'It is—definitely—time to go.'

She pushed back the thin quilt and got out of bed, running her fingers through her tousled light brown hair, smoothing it into its usual shoulder-length bob. That was one thing she had refused to economise on—her monthly trip to the best hairdresser in town.

There were shadows under her long-lashed hazel eyes, she realised, giving herself a swift, critical glance in the mirror, and the flowered cotton pyjamas she'd bought from a market stall covered her slim body without grace.

She felt, she recognised with bewilderment, like a stranger in her own skin. A being totally alien to the cherished, pampered girl she'd been eighteen months ago. That girl had vanished for ever.

Her mouth tightened with sudden bleakness. But there was no time to linger feeling sorry for herself, she thought, squaring her shoulders. Kit had phoned the previous evening to call an emergency breakfast meeting at the Children's Centre, and she couldn't be late.

She collected clean underwear, and one of the plain grey skirts and cream blouses that formed her working gear, and headed for the small dank shower room which had been created in a corner of the attic room she inhabited.

The landlord had thrown up cheap plywood partitions to divide the living space from the sleeping area, and pushed together a rudimentary kitchen with a sink and a gas stove in an alcove. He felt that entitled him to christen the whole thing a flat, but it was still nothing more than a draughty bedsit.

To call it adequate would pay it an undeserved compliment, Cally thought, grimacing over the fact that her towel was still damp from the day before.

It was not the kind of accommodation she had ever envisaged for herself. But it was just affordable, and it was also the last place on earth where anyone would think to look for her, and that was its major—its sole—attraction for her as far as she was concerned.

Still she would bid it goodbye without a moment's regret.

Although she couldn't say the same for Wellingford itself, oddly enough.

She'd chosen it for the same reasons she'd picked the flat. It was a small, nondescript market town beside an unexciting river. A neutral background that she could disappear into. Somewhere to provide her with breathing space to think and consider her long-term future.

She had not expected to like it, of course, Cally thought,

trying to coax hot water out of the reluctant shower. She had certainly not anticipated being happy here either, yet somehow, against all the odds, she'd achieved a measure of both.

There were times when she'd almost managed to forget her reasons for being there. Almost, but not quite.

And now it was time to leave, she told herself. She'd already stayed more than a month over her allotted time, and she simply couldn't risk remaining any longer. Otherwise she might start to feel at home, and that was dangerous. She needed to keep moving. To cover her tracks.

Although there was no actual proof that this was necessary, she reminded herself. No evidence of any attempt to trace her, as she'd feared. She could well be panicking unduly. Yet some gut instinct—some sense of self-preservation—seemed to be warning her again. Otherwise, why the dreams?

In any case, there were valid, practical reasons for her to leave Wellingford.

For one thing, the job she'd enjoyed so much no longer existed, and at the end of the week she would receive her final wage packet from the Hartley family. Who would begrudge her every penny of it.

She sighed as she cleaned her teeth. She could still hardly believe that Genevieve Hartley was dead. She'd seemed indomitable—eternal. Even now, six weeks later, Cally half expected to see the large car draw up at the end of Gunners Wharf and Mrs Hartley's small, silver-haired figure alight.

Riding to our rescue, Cally thought grimacing. Except it was far too late for that.

I hope the dead can't see the living, she told herself with sudden fierceness. I hope Mrs Hartley doesn't know what her ghastly sons and their expensive wives did to her dream for Gunners Wharf even before she was cold in her grave. All those hopes and plans and hard work just swept away. All those people suddenly discovering they needed somewhere else to live.

It shouldn't have happened, of course. Mrs Hartley's intentions had been very different. She'd meant the Gunners Wharf project to survive and thrive even when she was no longer there to supervise it. She'd been to see her lawyers, to draw up the necessary adjustments to her will, only to succumb to a sudden devastating heart attack before the all-important document could be signed.

Even so, the residents had all hoped that her wishes would be respected. She'd made them clear enough even to her resentful children.

So they'd collected for a wreath, and attended the funeral to demonstrate their affection and respect for the woman who'd encouraged their visions, only to find themselves totally ignored by the family, their presence unnecessary and embarrassing.

A bad omen, Cally had thought at the time, unease twisting inside her.

And her premonition had been quite correct.

Within two weeks all the tenants had received notice to quit, and Gunners Wharf had been sold for redevelopment. They'd protested, naturally, but legally, they'd been told, they didn't have a leg to stand on. Their leases had been privately agreed with Mrs Hartley, and the rents kept deliberately, unrealistically low.

But there'd been nothing in writing, and her sudden death had prevented her from regularising their position in law.

Besides, it had been added, in a final blow to their hopes, most of the houses were still waiting to be renovated, and could well be deemed unfit for human habitation.

As she put on her clothes Cally tasted the acid of tears in her throat, and swallowed them back. She'd become genuinely fond of Genevieve Hartley, and her death had been a personal blow, quite apart from all the other ramifications.

On the other hand, the abandonment of the Gunners Wharf housing project would give Cally a personal release.

I always knew my time here was limited, she reminded herself, applying moisturiser to her pale skin. But I thought I'd be the first to leave.

Once again someone she loved had been suddenly and tragically taken away from her. And once again she was left floundering in a kind of limbo.

Genevieve Hartley had been almost the first person Cally had met when she'd arrived in Wellingford.

She'd been sitting in the bus station buffet, drinking coffee while she looked through the small ads in the local weekly paper, scanning them for job opportunities and room rentals, when she'd spotted the last entry in the 'Situations Vacant' column.

'Administrative assistant required for housing project with Children's Centre,' she'd read. 'Enthusiastic and computer literate. Able to work on own initiative.' Followed by a telephone number.

Less than an hour later she'd been in Mrs Hartley's elegant drawing room, being interviewed.

She'd been unfazed to find that her future employer was a chic elderly woman with steely blue eyes and an autocratic manner. She was used to ageing despots. In fact, she'd spent most of her life with one, she thought ruefully. So Mrs Hartley's brisk, searching interrogation had come as no real shock.

Cally had sat composedly, answering the older woman's questions with quiet candour.

Yes, she had references, but mainly for waitressing and shop work. She'd been taking a kind of gap year, she'd added, mentally crossing her fingers, travelling around and working at whatever jobs offered themselves.

'But you have worked with computers?' Genevieve Hartley poured China tea into thin porcelain cups. 'I need someone who can do word processing, keep records and oversee the on-going renovation scheme. Also act as liaison between the builders, the tenants and the Town Hall.' She paused with a faint smile. 'My tenants at Gunners Wharf have not had easy starts in life, and this has made them wary, so sometimes the situation can become—shall we say volatile? I'm looking for someone who can sort out any snags before they become real difficulties.'

Cally hesitated. 'I took computer studies during my last year at school.'

'Which school was that?'

Cally told her, and the plucked brows rose. 'Indeed?' said Genevieve Hartley. 'Then I suggest a fortnight's trial on both sides. After all,' she added drily, 'you might find some of the tenants rather too much of a problem.'

I'd find not eating a much greater one, Cally thought wryly. Thought it but did not say it.

'In addition to the administrative work you'll be asked to take your turn at the Children's Centre, particularly helping out in the coffee bar.' She gave Cally an unexpectedly sweet smile. 'So your past experience could be useful, my dear.'

The money Mrs Hartley had offered was reasonable, but not lavish. It had enabled Cally to live, yet hadn't encouraged her to put down roots. Which was exactly what she needed.

In time, when she was entirely free of her former life, she would find a home, and a career. Until then she would continue to be a nomad, because it was safer that way.

Tonight, she thought, adding a muted lustre to her lips, she would get out her map book and decide where to go next.

The river might sparkle in the sunshine, but the brightness did no favours to the dilapidated warehouses and crumbling sheds along Gunners Wharf itself.

In many ways redevelopment was exactly what was needed for the entire area, Cally conceded reluctantly as she walked down to the Centre, where the admin office was based. But why did it have to happen at the expense of the housing scheme? Why couldn't they have existed side by side?

Here, in the back street running parallel to the wharf, nearly half the properties had already been restored, with new windows and roofs, freshly pointed brickwork and gleaming paint. A lot of the work had been done by the tenants themselves, as an act of faith—an investment in a future that had now been taken from them, she thought bleakly.

Mrs Hartley had provided the Children's Centre at her own

expense, patiently providing funds to meet every new Health and Safety regulation that the local council could throw at them. It was no secret that it had cost her a small fortune, and maybe this was what her sons had resented so much. Because it was also known that Hartleys department store, like many other High Street shops, had been struggling for a couple of years, and needed a cash injection.

Well, they certainly had it now, Cally thought, biting her lip. The sale had gone through so fast that they must have had a string of potential buyers already lined up. While the single mothers and families in badly paid work they were turning out would struggle to find alternative housing that they could afford.

She sighed. But, as her grandfather had always said, one man's gain was another's loss. And the whole scheme had been living on borrowed time anyway.

'Cally.' A girl's voice broke across her reverie, and she turned to see Tracy approaching, pushing her baby buggy over the dilapidated pavement. 'Cally—what's this meeting about? Do you know? Has Kit said anything?'

Cally stifled a sigh, and pulled a silly face at the baby in the pushchair, an act rewarded by a lopsided grin.

'Not a thing,' she responded briskly. 'But we don't live in each other's pockets, you know.'

She'd said it before so often, but no one seemed to take her denials seriously. Kit Matlock was the director of the Centre, and the man with whom she worked most closely. They were both, on the face of it, single, so assumptions were made.

Nor could Cally deny that, before the recent bombshell, Kit had been making it clear he'd like to shift their professional relationship to a more personal level—which was, in itself, another excellent reason for moving away.

Not that she disliked him. How could she? He was attractive, pleasant, and endearingly short on temperament. But they were not an item, and never would be. And Cally had resolutely made excuse after excuse to refuse his invitations.

Their most intimate involvement to date had only been the

sharing of sandwiches and coffee at lunchtime, in her small, crowded office at the rear of the Centre. And that was as far as it would ever go.

Because, she told herself, I don't cheat.

'Oh,' Tracy said, obviously disappointed. 'I thought maybe he'd found a loophole in the law or something. And obviously he'd tell you first.'

Cally buried her bare hands in the pockets of her black jacket and forced a smile. 'You're barking up the wrong tree, Tracy—honestly. Kit's a lovely guy, but I'm moving on very soon. I've been offered another job—in London,' she added with sudden inspiration.

Tracy stared at her, woebegone. 'You're leaving?'

'I have to. Technically, I'm unemployed, so I need to find work pretty urgently.' Kit too, she thought.

Tracy groaned. 'It's all falling apart,' she said dismally.

Cally felt intensely sorry for her. Tracy's house had been one of the first in the terrace to be overhauled. There had been serious damp in the upstairs rooms, and little Brad had been seeing a local doctor with non-stop chest complaints. Now he was well enough to use the Centre, and Tracy had found part-time work as a supermarket checkout assistant. Things had been looking up for both of them. Now the coin was in the air again.

Most of the others were already there, hunched awkwardly on miniature chairs in the playroom, drinking coffee and nibbling half-heartedly on the Danish pastries Kit had brought.

The air of gloom was almost tangible as he stood up. 'Sorry to drag you here so early, everyone. I asked for this meeting because, thanks to Leila, we now know who's bought Gunners Wharf.'

There was a murmur of surprise. 'How did you manage that?' someone asked.

Leila looked round with open complacency. 'My mum's next door neighbour works in the planning department at the Town Hall. The company's called Eastern Crest Developments, and they're going to be in town the day after tomorrow. Roy says they're putting on an exhibition at the Town Hall to show how they're going to redevelop Gunners Wharf with the Council.' She nodded. 'So this is our chance.'

'To do what?' Cally asked.

'To show them they can't just walk all over us,' Leila informed her triumphantly. 'I say we picket the Town Hall. Carry banners saying "Save our Homes" and "Hands off Gunners Wharf". Chain ourselves to the railings if necessary.'

Cally groaned inwardly. 'Why stop there?' she said. 'Why not march down the High Street and put a brick through Hartleys' windows?'

Leila's eyes widened. 'Hey, that's not a bad idea.'

'You're right,' Cally said shortly. 'It's more than bad. It's appalling—and illegal as well.'

'Well,' Leila said defiantly, 'so is what they've done to us.'

'I was going to suggest a slightly softer approach,' said Kit. 'Why don't a few of us go to the exhibition and actually talk to the developers? See if their scheme couldn't be adapted somehow to include Gunners Terrace. Suggest it could show the human side of big business. After all, they may not even know we exist down here. I bet the Hartleys won't have mentioned it during negotiations,' he added grimly.

There were a couple of upturned noses. 'I've heard it's all going to be yuppie flats and designer boutiques,' someone said. 'They won't want the likes of us making the place look untidy.'

'And won't this Town Hall thing be invitation only?' another voice asked.

'Well, Roy could get us the invites,' said Leila.

'And it has to be worth a try, surely?' added Tracy.

Kit gave her a warm smile. 'I certainly think so.' He paused. 'Maybe you should be part of the deputation, with Cally and myself.'

'Just three?' Leila queried with a touch of belligerence.

'I think small could be beautiful under the circumstances,' Kit said smoothly. 'No use going in mob-handed. That could be seen as aggressive, and we want a discussion, not a confrontation.' He paused. 'Of course we'll be relying on you for the entry passes.'

There was a silence while Leila weighed her own disgruntlement against the good of the Gunners Terrace community as a whole. At last, 'Not a problem,' she said grudgingly, and there was a collective sigh of relief.

'Is it really necessary for me to go?' Cally asked later, when she and Kit were momentarily alone.

Kit shrugged. 'If we manage to talk to Eastern Crest's big bosses, it would be useful to have an accurate note of what's said.'

'Tracy could do that.'

He shook his head. 'Tracy gets flustered, and she's too involved to be objective anyway. She'll hear what she wants to hear. Besides, she's there for the sympathy vote,' he added, grimacing slightly. 'Pretty blonde single mother, whose baby used to be always ailing. That might tug at their hard heartstrings.'

'Good PR—if slightly callous.' Cally doodled aimlessly with a pencil. 'What do you think the chances are?'

'Of getting them to listen? Pretty good—especially without Leila threatening to kneecap them. Overall?' He shook his head. 'I'm not hopeful. Major property companies are moneymakers, after all, not social workers.'

'Yes,' Cally said quietly. 'They're generally not famous for their humanitarian qualities. They tend to have their own agenda.'

'Therefore,' Kit went on, 'we need to present our case in an articulate and reasonable way—and pray like hell.' He paused. 'Of course, what we really need is a *deus ex machina*—another rich philanthropist to make a counter-offer and save us all at the eleventh hour.' He grinned at her. 'Got many millionaires in your address book?'

The pencil snapped suddenly in her fingers. 'No,' she said, her voice faintly hoarse. 'Not many.'

'Nor me,' he acknowledged ruefully, and was silent for a moment. When he spoke, his voice was hesitant. 'After the meeting, we could maybe have some dinner—at that Italian place in the High Street. What do you think?'

'Fine by me,' Cally agreed. 'But you'd better warn Tracy to get a babysitter,' she added disingenuously. 'It will do her good to get out for the evening.'

Kit's face fell a little, but he knew better than to argue.

When she was by herself again, Cally wondered whether that would have been a good time to tell him she was leaving—if he hadn't guessed already. After all, the Hartleys must have him under notice too, although they'd reluctantly agreed to let the Children's Centre remain open for the time being.

They're thinking of nasty stories appearing in the local paper, Cally thought. Television cameras filming weeping children in pushchairs. The kind of publicity one's friendly local department store needs like a hole in the head.

The kids' parents, of course, were a different matter. Not everyone had the same concern for the disadvantaged as Genevieve Hartley had had, or tried to do anything about it. They'd be counting on that.

And the Gunners Terrace residents, once they were made homeless, would qualify for council housing anyway. That would be their argument, so how many people would really care if a small, struggling would-be community fell by the wayside?

But Cally knew that real pride, real spirit was being engendered in this tiny part of town, where those qualities had long been absent. And that it mattered. But it would soon wane once the families were dispersed, as seemed inevitable.

They deserve to survive, she told herself with sudden angry passion. They don't need another defeat. If only—*only*—there was something I could do…

But there could have been—once, a sly voice in her head reminded her. If you'd chosen another kind of life. If you hadn't run away. You might have made all the difference.

For a moment she was motionless, staring into the distance with eyes that saw nothing but pain.

She said under her breath, 'But I made the right—the only possible choice. I know that.' And dropped the broken pencil into the wastepaper basket.

She had no smart clothes, so she opted for another version of her working gear for their visit to the Town Hall.

The exhibition, which included a video presentation as well as a scale model of the development, was being staged in the conference hall—which hadn't seen many conferences, but was useful for antiques fairs and craft markets. Also for the flower show in its usual inclement weather.

The Mayor and his entourage were clearly preening themselves because the place was living up to its grandiose title at last.

There were a lot of people present, most of them clustered around the tables where the scale model was set up, and the remainder hovering near the lavish buffet.

Waiters were going round with trays of champagne and heavy platters loaded with canapés, presumably all with the compliments of Eastern Crest. How to win friends and influence people, Cally thought cynically as she stood with Kit and Tracy, wondering whom they should approach.

But in the end the decision was made for them when they found themselves caught in a pincer movement by Gordon Hartley and his younger brother Neville, their faces flushed and inimical as they strode across the room.

'I wasn't aware anyone had asked you here.' Gordon addressed Kit, ignoring the two girls completely. 'I'd like you to leave—now.'

Kit held up three invitation cards. 'Someone clearly has a different idea,' he returned coolly. 'I thought we should see what we're up against.'

'You're up against nothing,' Neville chimed in. 'You've already lost, so what's the point in coming here, making fools of yourselves? Our mother may have looked on you all as an act of charity, but we don't.'

'All the same.' Kit was undeterred. 'We'd like to have a

look at the proposed development, and maybe speak to whoever's in charge at Eastern Crest.'

Cally found herself admiring his calmness. His refusal to be rattled. He had 'We shall not be moved' written all over him, in spite of the hostility he was faced with.

Goodness, she thought, if Leila had come she'd have bitten someone in the leg by now.

'Then you're really out of luck.' Gordon was speaking again, his tone curt, pushing his weight forward threateningly. 'Because the chairman himself is hosting tonight's presentation, and he plays in the big league. Get out now, before you become a laughing stock or he has you removed.'

The brothers' raised voices were attracting attention, Cally realised, with embarrassment. Curious glances from all over the room were coming their way, and even some of the crowd round the model were turning their heads to look.

She realised that she wasn't just uncomfortable, she'd actually begun to tremble inside. Even begun to be afraid in some obscure but compelling way.

We shouldn't be here, she thought, swallowing. We may have invitations, but there'll be an official guest list somewhere, and we're still gatecrashers.

She touched Kit's sleeve. 'Listen,' she began, 'maybe we should…'

But the sentence was never completed. Because she was suddenly aware that a hush had fallen. That someone was making his way across the room towards them between groups of people that obediently fell back at his approach.

A tall man, she saw, with a thin tanned face under fashionably dishevelled hair, dark as a raven's wing. A face marked by high cheekbones, a nose and chin almost arrogant in their strength, a mouth tough and unsmiling. And totally unforgettable.

The muscularity of his broad-shouldered, lean-hipped body was emphasised by the elegance of his designer suit as he strode towards them with powerful, determined grace, purpose in his every line.

He was someone, she realised, the breath catching in her throat, that she knew. Whose reappearance in her life she'd been dreading for over a year. And who was here now, almost within touching distance, when there was no time to run or place to go.

All she could do was stand her ground and pray to whatever unseen deity protected fugitives.

But as his eyes, grey and deep as a winter ocean, met hers, Cally felt the measure of his glance in the marrow of her bones, and knew that her escape had only been an illusion all along.

'Good evening.' The cool, crisp voice was like ice on her skin. 'Is there some problem?'

A game, Cally thought numbly. He was playing a game, with rules that he'd invented. But no one knew it but herself.

'A few troublemakers have got in, Sir Nicholas,' Neville Hartley said swiftly. 'But we're dealing with them. So if you'd like to go back to your guests...'

'Presently,' the newcomer said quietly. He looked at Kit. 'May I know who you are?'

Kit cleared his throat. 'I'm Christopher Matlock, and I run the Children's Centre, and the Residents' Association down at Gunners Wharf. We face eviction because of your development, but I'm still hoping some compromise can be reached, and that you might spare me some time to discuss the matter.'

'Ah, yes.' The other man nodded. 'This has been mentioned to me.' He turned to Tracy, whose face had been blotched with nerves ever since their arrival. 'And this is?' His smile held a swift charm that softened the hardness of his face.

'Tracy—Tracy Andrews,' Kit said quickly, seeing that she was beyond speech. 'One of the residents.' He turned to Cally. 'And this is my administrative assistant.'

'Oh, but we need no introduction,' the new arrival said with cold mockery. 'Do we, Caroline, my love?'

Before she could move he took one long step towards her, capturing her chin in his long fingers. He bent his head, and for a brief, hideous second Cally felt the sear of his mouth on hers.

He straightened, his lips twisting. 'They say absence makes the heart grow fonder. I wonder if that's true. Because you don't seem very pleased to see me.'

'Cally?' Kit was staring at her, lips parted in shock. 'You know this man?'

'Yes.' She forced her lips to move to make the necessary sounds. 'His name is Nicholas Tempest.'

'I'm the chairman of Eastern Crest.' His smile did not reach his eyes. The gaze that held hers was a challenge, and a warning. 'Now, tell him the rest, darling.'

And from some far, terrible distance, she heard herself say, with a kind of empty helplessness, 'He's my husband.'

CHAPTER TWO

THERE was a moment when she thought she might faint. When she would have welcomed the temporary surcease to this intolerable moment that unconsciousness would provide.

But she wasn't that lucky.

Instead she heard Nick drawl, 'Will someone fetch a chair for my wife? She's had a shock.'

It was exactly the challenge she needed. I am not—*not*—going to fall apart, she told herself, her body stiffening. At least not now.

She made her tone crisp. 'Thank you, but I'm perfectly all right.'

She turned to Kit, who was looking poleaxed, while Tracy was standing with her mouth open and her eyes out on stalks.

'But please get Tracy a drink,' she added. 'She really needs one.' She took a deep breath. 'I think it's best if I leave.'

'Not yet, darling.' Nick's voice was silky, but the fingers that closed on her wrist felt like iron. 'After all, you went to the trouble of seeking me out tonight. So why don't you say what you came to say?'

Cally bit her lip. It was her left hand that he'd imprisoned. The hand that had once, for a few hours, worn his ring but was now bare—a fact, she could tell, that wasn't lost on him.

She wanted to pull free, but feared an undignified struggle which she might lose. She said brusquely, 'Kit's our spokesman. Perhaps he could make an appointment to see you tomorrow.'

'Unfortunately I shall be leaving after breakfast.' He paused. 'But I could spare you all some time later, when tonight's presentation is over.'

'But we're going out for a meal.' The champagne she was

sipping seemed to have loosened Tracy's tongue. 'An Italian meal. My neighbour's looking after the baby,' she added, beaming.

'Then why don't I join you?' Nick suggested, smoothly and unanswerably. 'You can put forward your point of view over veal Marsala.'

Tracy stared at him. 'But I was going to have lasagne.'

'Then of course you shall.' He was smiling again, using that charm of his like a weapon. Controlling the tense silence that had descended. 'While you tell me all about Gunners Terrace.'

'It was an idea of our late mother's,' Gordon Hartley butted in, almost desperately. 'Sadly, she died while the scheme was in its infancy, so most of the houses are still untouched. They're dangerous and insanitary, and they should be pulled down.'

In spite of her mental and emotional turmoil Cally managed to give him a steady look. 'That isn't altogether true, and you know it. Half the terrace has been completed, and work has started on the others.'

'But we won't talk about it here and now,' Nick cut in decisively. He'd released Cally's wrist, but the pressure of his fingers seemed to linger like a bruise. 'I still have things to do, so we'll have to postpone the discussion.'

'There's really nothing to talk about, Sir Nicholas,' Neville Hartley blustered. 'I think we've made the position quite clear already.'

'One side of it, certainly,' Nick agreed. He looked at Kit. 'What's the name of the restaurant you're using?'

'The Toscana,' Kit muttered awkwardly. 'In the High Street.'

Nick looked at his watch. 'Then I'll meet you there in an hour's time.' He paused. 'All of you,' he added softly, his gaze resting briefly on Cally. 'I hope that's clearly understood.' Another swift, hard smile and he was gone, and the crowd seemed to close round him.

There was a taut silence, and Cally could see the Hartley brothers exchanging wary glances.

She could understand their problem, she thought wryly. Young Lady Tempest, wife of Eastern Crest's dynamic chairman, would have been an honoured guest, overwhelmed with obsequious attention. Nick Tempest's clearly estranged wife was a horse of a different colour, and they weren't sure quite how to deal with her.

To be civil to someone who'd encouraged Genevieve Hartley in her reckless foolishness and battled with them openly after her death would be anathema, but neither could they throw her bodily into the street with her companions, as they obviously wished.

After all, Gunners Terrace was supposed to be down and out, just waiting for the bulldozers to arrive. Now the residents had an unsuspected ace up their sleeve, and for the moment the Hartleys didn't have a strategy to deal with it.

In the end Neville Hartley said thickly, 'You haven't heard the last of this.' And they stalked furiously away.

'Perhaps that should be our line,' Cally called after them, her voice inimical.

Then suddenly the tension went out of her, and she was gasping as if she'd been winded.

Kit was staring at her as if she was a stranger. 'I can't believe this,' he said. '*You* are married—to *him*? It can't be true.'

'It's perfectly true.' Her voice was raw. 'But not for much longer, I assure you. Once I've been separated from him—from Nick—for two years, divorce should be easy.'

'Is that how he sees it?' Kit asked sombrely.

'What do you mean?'

'You were the surprised one just now,' he said. 'If you ask me, your husband knew you were going to be here tonight, and he was waiting for you.'

'He's very dishy,' Tracy said on a note of envy. 'I wouldn't mind him waiting for me.'

Cally gave a taut smile. 'Well, at the restaurant you can have him all to yourself. I've had enough surprises for one day, and I'm going home.'

'But you can't,' Kit said, dismayed. 'You heard him. He's

willing to listen to what we have to say—something we hardly dared hope for. But it has to be all of us or it'll be no dice. Cally, you can't walk away—not when we actually have a chance to put our case.'

She looked down at the floor. 'I think I'd be more likely to damage your cause than help it.'

I should have listened to that dream the other night, she thought. Accepted it as a warning and gone while the going was good. But I was too complacent. I let myself think that he'd have stopped searching by now—if he'd ever begun.

Unless, of course, this is all one sick coincidence. But somehow I don't think so.

'If you're not with us, I don't think we'll have a cause,' Kit told her grimly. 'You can't give up on it all now. Besides, what point would there be when he knows where you are?'

It was logical—it was reasonable—but it made the situation no easier to accept.

She said, 'I can't just—meet him socially. Too much has happened.'

'Then look on it as a business meeting,' Kit urged. 'They say half the deals in the country are done in restaurants.'

She bent her head. 'You really think he's going to offer any concessions?'

'Why not? He didn't have to agree to talk to us. He could have insisted on seeing you alone. That's a hopeful sign, isn't it?'

'Nick likes to manipulate people,' she said. 'And he always has his own agenda.'

'Nevertheless,' he said stubbornly, 'it has to be worth a try.' He paused, and his tone altered. 'Cally—did you ever intend to tell me you were married?'

She gave him a straight look. 'I didn't plan to be around long enough for that to be necessary. Anyway, it's not an episode I'm proud of. I'm just thankful it will soon be over and done with.'

'Why's he a sir?' asked Tracy.

'Because he's a baronet. He inherited the title from a distant cousin.'

'With loads of land and money?' Tracy was clearly intrigued. 'That's dead romantic.'

'Most of the land had been sold off,' Cally said wearily. 'And he was already a millionaire several times over. So all he really got was a rather rundown house.'

'Was it love at first sight?' Tracy persisted. 'When you met him? I mean, you obviously fancied him enough to marry him.'

'Actually,' Cally said in a clear, bright voice, 'it was just a business arrangement. Only I decided rather late in the day that I couldn't go through with it after all. And I'd rather not talk about it any more either,' she added.

Except that she almost certainly wouldn't have a choice in the matter, she told herself, grabbing a glass of champagne from a passing tray and swallowing some of it down her dry throat.

Because she was faced at last with the confrontation she'd have given anything to avoid.

She tried not to look—to see where Nick was in the busy room, or if he was alone. Particularly that. She strove hard not to wonder what he was thinking—or what he might have to say to her later. Because there was bound to be some kind of reckoning.

Even if he agreed that a quick and quiet divorce was the best way out of their situation—and as far as Cally was concerned there was no possible alternative—she was still unlikely to escape totally unscathed.

I left him with a lot of explaining to do, she told herself tautly. Made him look a fool. Something he's unlikely to forgive or forget.

And now she would have to come up with an explanation for her headlong flight from him.

Not the truth, of course. That was locked away deep within her, and she would not go there. But something—anything—that would carry a modicum of conviction.

She put down her glass and with a murmured excuse went

out of the room, down a flight of stone steps to the women's cloakroom. She had it to herself, which she was grateful for, because one glance in the mirror told her that she looked as if she was running a temperature. Her eyes were feverishly bright, and there was a hectic flush along her cheekbones, so the last thing she wanted was for someone to ask if she was all right—especially if Nick was around to hear it.

I need to look cool, calm and collected, she told herself, as she ran the cold tap over the pounding pulses in her wrists and applied a damp tissue to her temples. I have to keep the emotional temperature low, no matter how difficult it may get later, because I can't afford any sign of weakness.

And if they could only agree to conduct the eventual divorce in a rational, equable spirit, that would be a bonus.

She supposed divorce was the solution. She couldn't imagine Nick accepting the annulment that represented the true state of affairs between them. Not good for his all-powerful male image, she thought wryly.

Although it would be her lack of sex appeal that would probably be blamed. What else could it be? Because, where women were concerned, Nick Tempest didn't have to prove a thing.

Whereas she—she had little to offer. She was still too thin, she admitted, and under normal circumstances too pale. Her features were generally nondescript, with that thick, glossy fall of hair her only real claim to beauty. Although even that was brown. The whole picture was dull and duller, underlined by a blouse, skirt and jacket that didn't hold a scrap of allure between them.

No change there, she thought, her mouth twisting.

The witnesses at their wedding must have imagined they were watching a peacock mate with an ugly duckling.

But then Nick hadn't married her for her attractions, or her charm. He'd had his own reasons...as she'd finally discovered, she thought, tension lancing her as those hidden memories stirred again.

Not that it mattered, she told herself vehemently. It was all past and done with, and soon that would be a matter of law.

I want nothing from him, she thought, but my freedom. And surely that isn't too much to ask? He should be glad to be rid of me at so little cost.

In these past strange months in limbo, she'd learned that she could earn sufficient to keep herself without luxuries. Once she was no longer running away, she could actually seek some training, prepare herself for a career. Life would open up in front of her.

And, however long it took, and however painful the process, she would learn to forget that for a few hours she'd been Nick Tempest's convenient bride.

'So you're still here.' Tracy came into the cloakroom. 'Kit sent me to find you. I think he was getting worried in case you'd disappeared.'

'No.' Cally had managed to tone down the worst of her flush with powder. She produced her comb and started to smooth her hair. 'I'm still around.'

'Put some lippy on,' Tracy suggested.

'I haven't brought any.' It was a fib, but she hadn't used it earlier, and there was no way she wanted to look as if she'd made any kind of effort. It was the kind of feminine detail that Nick would notice, she thought, with a pang.

'Kit thinks we should go and have a quiet drink at the White Hart.' Tracy went on. 'Plan our tactics, he says.' She gave Cally a straight look. 'You don't think there's much point, do you?'

Cally put her comb in her bag. She said quietly, 'I honestly don't know. He could simply have refused to talk to us.'

'Well, he's your husband, so you should know,' said Tracy. She added, 'And it's not really "us", at all. It's you—isn't it?' And her eyes met Cally's with a question she was unable to answer.

By the time they reached the restaurant Cally was on tenterhooks, totally gripped by tension. The preliminary discussion in the pub hadn't got very far, because Kit was clearly still upset about her concealed marriage and was prepared to be resentful, which she regretted.

She realised, to her shame, that she was hoping against hope that Nick would yield to the Hartleys' blandishments and not turn up.

You're supposed to be fighting for Gunners Terrace, she reproached herself silently. Balance that against an awkward hour or so in your ex-husband's company, and get a grip.

But Nick was there before them, occupying a corner table—the best in the house, naturally—and accompanied by a fair, stocky man whom he introduced as Matthew Hendrick, the project architect.

Cally was so determined not to sit next to Nick that she found herself placed opposite him instead, which was hardly an improvement, she thought, biting her lip with vexation.

While the menus were handed round, the bread brought and the wine poured, she could feel Nick's eyes on her in a cool assessment which she could not avoid and he did not even try to conceal.

She could only hope he was thanking his stars for a lucky escape, but her intuition warned her that she might be wrong.

She ate sparingly of the antipasti that formed the first course, and only picked at the chicken in its rich wine sauce that followed. She tried to fix her mind on the earnest discussion going on, primarily between Kit and Matthew Hendrick, while Nick watched and listened. This was all that should matter to her, she reminded herself. The plight of the residents. The need to save the project and continue it. She should be joining in here, making her own reasoned contribution, as Tracy was doing.

But she was too aware of the dark man opposite, with the cool, contained face. Too conscious of the apprehensive thoughts circling in her mind, giving her no peace.

She refused dessert and coffee, praying inwardly that the party would start to break up and she'd finally be let off the hook.

But it was a vain hope.

'Goodnight, Miss Andrews—Mr Matlock.' Nick had risen to

his feet and was shaking hands. 'Matthew, I'll meet you on site tomorrow at nine a.m. My wife and I are going to stay for a while, and enjoy our reunion.' His smile didn't reach his eyes. 'We have a lot of catching up to do—don't we, my sweet?'

Cally's lips parted to utter a startled protest, but she bit back the words and sank back in her chair. That same intuition told her that any resistance on her part would only make her look foolish in the end. Far better not to fuss, she thought, but to let him think she regarded spending time alone in his company with complete indifference.

But how that was to be achieved she hadn't the faintest idea.

The others left, and she saw Kit looking frowningly back at her. She was almost tempted to call out to him, ask him to stay, but she knew that wouldn't be fair. She'd enjoyed working with Kit, but she would never have wanted more even if she'd been free, and she would have told him goodbye without regrets.

Besides, if Eastern Crest were interested enough in what he had to say to hold a site meeting, she couldn't jeopardise that by allowing him to annoy the chairman.

And Nick had made his wishes coolly and brutally clear.

They were going to talk.

As he resumed his seat, she said in a small, brittle voice, 'I feel as if someone should read me my rights.'

'I already know mine,' he said shortly. 'I've had plenty of time to consider them.' He signalled to the waiter to bring more coffee.

'I don't want anything else,' she told him quickly.

'Then you can sit and chat to me while I have some. Doesn't that paint a nice domestic picture?'

'Nick,' she said, deciding to jump straight in, 'do we really have to do this? Can't we just accept that our marriage was a seriously bad idea and call it quits? I—I'd honestly like to go home.'

'An excellent idea,' he said affably. 'Why don't we do just that? Unfortunately, at the moment home for me happens to be the Majestic Hotel—a flagrant misnomer, if ever there was one.' He gave her a small, cold smile. 'I wonder if I could get them under the Trades Description Act? However,' he went on, 'with uncanny prescience, they've given me the bridal suite, so perhaps I should forgive their delusions of grandeur.' He drank down his espresso. 'Shall we go?'

She could suddenly feel the hectic drumming of her pulses. Hear the silent scream of *No* in her dry throat. She thought, He doesn't mean that. He can't...

Aloud, she said shakily, 'I'm going nowhere with you. You seem to have overlooked the fact that I've left you.'

'Oh, no, darling,' he said with corrosive lightness. 'I remember that incredibly well. Our wedding day, right? In fact, the ink was barely dry on the register when you scarpered.'

She said stiffly, 'I suppose you deserve some kind of explanation.'

'Yes,' he said, and his voice seemed to remove a layer of her skin. 'I bloody well do. And maybe an apology for making a fool of me quite so publicly. That would be a beginning.'

She bit her lip. 'Yes, of course. I—I'm sorry about that.'

'But nothing else?' Nick divined grimly.

She thought, *You were making a fool of me in private—or does that not count?*

She lifted her chin. 'It was something I had to do. I felt I had no choice.' She hesitated. 'What—what did you tell people?'

'I couldn't manage the truth,' he said. 'Because I didn't know what it was. I had no farewell note—no ''Dear John'' blotched with penitent tears to point me in the right direction. So I simply let it be known that you'd had a change of heart, however late in the day, and that we'd agreed to separate.'

He paused. 'You see, my sweet, at first I didn't realise what had happened. You'd taken the car, so originally I assumed there'd been an accident. I wasted a hell of a lot of time making increasingly frantic hospital calls, until the police called to say they'd picked up some kids joy-riding. They'd stolen your car from a station car park twenty miles away and written it off. The guy in the ticket office there recognised you from our engagement photograph—now, there's an irony—and said you'd bought a ticket to London. One way.' His mouth twisted harshly. 'That, of course, put an entirely new slant on the situation.'

Cally looked down at the tablecloth, tracing meaningless patterns on the white linen with her forefinger. 'So you did—go looking for me?'

'No,' he said. 'Not at first. Frankly, I was too bloody angry. So I thought, To hell with it. And her.'

'You should have left it like that.'

'Ah,' he said softly. 'But I too underwent a change of heart.'

There was a loaded silence, then she said jerkily, 'How—how did you know where to find me?'

'Except for those first weeks, I've always known where to find you.'

A shiver chilled her spine, and she closed her eyes momentarily. 'And I thought I'd managed to cover my tracks. That if I kept moving I'd drop out of sight.'

'Oh, finding you was the easy part,' he said sardonically. 'Deciding what to do about it was trickier.' He paused. 'There was a time, you see, when I thought you might come back. That you might find living with me marginally preferable to slaving away in various greasy spoons.' The grey eyes met hers. 'But you never did.'

'No,' she said. 'Because I thought I was free. It never occurred to me that I was simply on the end of a long rope.'

There was a silence, then he said, 'What made you come here?'

She shrugged. 'It's the same as any other place. And it seemed—anonymous.'

He said drily, 'It's about to undergo a revival. Someone's decided the town has commuter possibilities. Hence Gunners Wharf.'

'And hence your presence here, too.' Her voice was taut.

'It seemed too good an opportunity to miss,' he said slowly, and she knew he was not referring to the development. Or not solely. And felt her heartbeat falter in panic.

She said hurriedly, 'Eastern Crest—is that a new acquisition? I didn't recognise the name...'

'Well, darling,' he drawled, 'you haven't been around much, keeping up. And without you to divert my attention I've had more time to devote to acquisitions and mergers.' He paused. 'And if you'd recognised the name, you'd have done—what?'

There was another silence, then she said wearily, 'I don't know. Running and trying to hide has clearly been futile. And I suppose we needed to meet eventually, to discuss what to do about the divorce. But why at this particular time?'

'I was told you were seeing someone,' Nick said expressionlessly. 'So it seemed an opportune moment to intervene. Your colleague, Mr Matlock, appeared upset to hear you were married,' he added pensively. 'I do hope, darling, you haven't been making promises you're not entitled to keep.'

'I'm "seeing" no one,' Cally said through gritted teeth. 'And Kit has no reason to feel aggrieved. So you could have easily saved yourself the inconvenience.'

'Yet, as you say, we needed to meet—to talk about the future. So this became the time—and the place.' His smile was brief and without warmth. 'And apart from the implicit defiance in your voice and body language, you've hardly changed at all, my love.'

'Perhaps the defiance was always there,' she said. 'But you didn't notice.'

'I noticed a hell of a lot,' he said quietly. 'And I was prepared to make allowances. Only you never gave me that chance. You preferred to bolt as if I was some kind of mad axe murderer.'

'No,' she said. 'Nothing so dramatic. Simply because I wasn't going to live my life on your terms.'

His brows lifted. 'Did I impose any conditions? I can't recall them.'

'You made me become your wife,' she said, her throat tightening. 'That involves—obligations.'

'Ah,' he said softly. 'In plain words, you didn't want to sleep with me.' He gave her a meditative look. 'Admittedly, we didn't have a conventional courtship, but you never gave the impression at the time that you found me particularly repulsive.'

Cally bit her lip. 'Well, you know now.'

'In fact,' Nick went on, as if she hadn't spoken, 'there were moments when the indications seemed distinctly favourable. Or did I imagine that?'

No, thought Cally, a tide of unwilling colour rising in her face. You didn't imagine it—damn you.

She said stiffly, 'You'd naturally prefer to think so, of course. You wouldn't want a dent in that irresistible image of yours.'

'If I'd ever been conceited enough to entertain such a notion,' he returned icily, 'you'd have shattered it for ever when you ran away.'

'But I'm sure you've had consolation,' she flung at him, and could have bitten out her tongue. *She had not meant to say that.*

'Why, darling—' Nick's tone changed to mockery '—did you really expect me to soothe my wounded feelings by staying celibate?'

'And do you really expect me to care—one way or the other?'

As long as I'm not there to see it...

The thought flashed, unbidden, and was instantly suppressed. Even to admit as much damaged the mental and emotional barriers she'd so carefully constructed against him, and she couldn't afford that.

In fact, she couldn't afford any of this...

She took a deep breath. 'Nick—let's stop here and now, or we shall only say things we'll regret. Why don't we just—draw a line, let our respective lawyers deal with the rest of it?'

'Because you're assuming,' he said, 'that I share your wish for a divorce.'

She said, slowly and unsteadily, 'You can't mean that. You can't wish to stay married to someone who—who won't—live with you.'

'Of course not.' He sounded almost brisk. 'Naturally I want a wife who'll share my home and my bed.' He smiled at her, his eyes touching her—stripping her, she realised, as her heart began to flutter in panic.

'In fact, I want you, my sweet,' he added softly. 'Come back to me, and in return for your charming—and willing—company, I'll tell Matthew Hendrick to save your precious terrace and include it in the development. Turn me down, however, and the demolition crew move in next week. And that's my final word.'

He paused. 'So the future of Gunners Terrace rests entirely with you, darling.'

'You can't do this,' Cally protested, her voice hoarse with incredulity. 'You're making me responsible for other people's lives—other people's happiness. It—it's emotional blackmail.'

'Now, my viewpoint is slightly different,' he said. 'Because you stood beside me in church and made certain vows. I remember it perfectly. You were wearing a white dress with a lot of little buttons down the front of it. Frankly, I was fantasising about undoing them all—with my teeth,' he added, with a kind of sensuous reminiscence that made her shiver. 'Now, at last, I want those vows fulfilled, and I really think, my sweet, that I've waited long enough. Even you must agree that our wedding night is long overdue.'

She said numbly, 'You mean you'd—you'd actually force me to—to...'

'I've no intention of using force,' he told her coolly. 'It's high time that delightful body of yours discovered what it was made for. And, if memory serves, the last time you were in my arms you thought so too.'

Her head went back sharply, as if he had struck her. 'What you're suggesting is obscene. Unthinkable. You can't think for one moment that I'd agree.'

Nick shrugged. 'You came here tonight, Cally, of your own free will, wanting a favour. Quite a sizeable one at that. I'm now telling you the price ticket it carries. Whether you pay it, of course, is your choice alone. It depends on how strongly you feel about the survival of Gunners Terrace—these people you claim to care about so deeply.'

'You think I'll save them at the expense of my own life?'

'Not the whole of it,' he said. 'Just the year you stole from me when you ran away. You see, I still have use for you, and that should be enough time for you to repay some of the debt you owe me—and give me what I want.'

She moistened her lips with the tip of her tongue. 'I don't understand. You're saying now that you want me to come back to you, but only for a limited period?'

He said quietly, 'Just as long as it takes for you to give me a child. So make your mind up quickly, because the staff here are waiting to close.'

She stared at him, stunned and incredulous, her brain churning wildly. She was dazedly aware that what he'd said was correct. The other tables had emptied while they were talking and she hadn't even noticed. The waiters were gathered now in a small group at the end of the room, chatting amongst themselves.

While she sat in this pool of lamplight, like a fly trapped in amber... Listening to him, but not believing what she was hearing. She heard herself laugh, the sound strained and alien.

She said, mastering her voice somehow, 'You want me—to have your baby? You can't honestly be serious. It's ludicrous. Totally impossible.'

'Ah,' he said, 'but I am perfectly serious. This is a question of inheritance, Cally. I want an heir—someone to come after me. Son or daughter. I don't mind,' he added with a curt shrug.

'And that's good and sufficient reason...?' She choked over the words.

'I inherited Wylstone Hall because I was Ranald Tempest's only relative,' he said. 'But we were almost complete strangers to each other. 'Whatever I leave will damned well go to my own flesh and blood. Not some distant relation—someone I've barely met.'

He paused. 'Achieve this one thing for me, Cally, and then I'll release you from the marriage. I won't fight the divorce. In fact, I'll make it easy for you.' He paused. 'And you'll find me generous.'

Money, she thought. He means money. I'd probably never have to work again unless I wished it.

'And afterwards?' she asked, her voice shaking. 'If I should—have a child, what happens then?'

'That's open to negotiation,' he told her curtly. 'But I suggest that in principle we share joint custody. At first, anyway.'

She stared back at him. She said faintly, 'You must be—insane.'

'Why? Because I want my wife to have my baby? It seems a fairly normal course of events to me.'

'But we don't have a normal marriage.'

'Not at this moment, perhaps,' he said softly. 'But all that could change very soon.'

She said in a low voice, 'Is that—why you married me? Because you thought I was young and strong, and you could breed from me?'

Nick shrugged. 'We all have our own priorities,' he said. 'But rest assured that I also found you—highly desirable.'

Her arms went round her body in an involuntary gesture of self-protection, and she saw his mouth twist.

She said hurriedly, 'But surely there are other women...' She paused, swallowing. Trying to blot certain forbidden images from her mind. 'I mean—you could divorce me quickly and find someone else. Someone who'd make you happy. Want to give you a family.'

'Let me be blunt,' he said. 'I've had time to think during our—separation, and I've discovered I've no real taste for being a husband. One unlucky foray into matrimony is quite enough, and I have no plans to replace you.' His faint smile was cynical. 'Don't they say, "Better the devil you know"?'

'Yes,' she said numbly. 'Sometimes—they do.' *But it doesn't have to be true.*

'Besides, you clearly can't wait to get away from me,' he added. 'So there's no threat of you wanting to hang around on a permanent basis.'

She said tautly, 'Cramping your style?'

'Precisely, darling,' he drawled. 'How well you're getting to know me.'

'Then think about this instead,' Cally pressed on, with a touch of desperation. 'There's no certainty about these things. Pregnancy and the rest of it. For all we know I might not—one of us might not—be able to have children.'

Nick shrugged. 'That's a risk I'm prepared to take.' His eyes met hers. 'Are you on the Pill?'

Mutely, she shook her head. A celibate life, she thought, didn't need that kind of protection.

'Then I'd need you to guarantee to stay off it,' he said curtly. 'But the final decision, as I've made clear, rests entirely with you. You either co-operate—come back to me as my wife—or you don't. A simple choice.'

Simple? Cally thought, a bubble of hysteria forming in her chest. *Simple?* Was that what he really believed?

'It's revenge—isn't it?' Her voice was torn—ragged. 'You want to punish me—humiliate me. It's payback time.'

'If so, you're heavily in arrears, sweetheart,' he told her unsmilingly. 'Tell me something, Cally, why accept my marriage proposal in the first place—if it was so degrading to you?'

She hesitated warily. 'I—I suppose I was grateful. It was all a hell of a mess and you rescued us. Although you had no reason to do so. And if I never said it before, I'll say it now. Thank you for that—for everything you did for my grandfather—and for me.'

His glance was cynical. 'I want more than words, Cally.'

Her voice trembled. 'But I have nothing else to give. I could try and repay you in other ways eventually, but I won't—do what you want. You must see that. I—I can't...'

He studied her for a moment, brows raised, then reached into his jacket for a mobile phone.

'What are you doing?'

'Calling Matt at the hotel, to tell him tomorrow's site visit is cancelled.' His voice was clipped. 'You can tell the residents why any deal's off. You have the rest of the night to plan your explanation. I suggest you make it a good one, because according to your boyfriend a lot of lives are going to be devastated. I'd hate for them to blame you, but I suspect they might.'

'No.' It hurt to breathe suddenly. 'Wait.'

'Well?' The response was uncompromising, the phone still in his hand.

She looked down at her fingers, laced tightly together in her lap.

'Gunners Terrace is precious to me,' she said tautly. 'Perhaps more than I'd even realised. And so is my eventual freedom.' She paused. 'I presume you're also prepared to guarantee that—in writing?'

'If that's what it takes.' Nick put the phone back in his pocket.

She lifted her head. Met his gaze directly. Unflinchingly. 'Then I'll—do what you want. But you have to give me some time—some space—to adjust.'

'And why should I do that?' He sounded almost casually interested.

She said, quietly and clearly, 'Because I don't want my only child to be—made in hatred. And I don't believe you'd want that either.'

'You really think you hate me?' Faint, galling amusement in his voice.

She nodded. 'I know it.'

'So what are you suggesting instead?' he drawled. 'Surely not—love?'

She winced. 'I thought—some kind of compromise. After all, you were prepared once to make allowances—you said so earlier.'

'How unwise of me.' He was silent for a moment. 'Very well. I've had a year to practise restraint, so I suppose I can go on being patient for a while.'

He signalled for the bill, then turned back to her, the grey eyes merciless. 'But be warned, darling. Don't push your luck.

Because I have no intention of waiting for ever. Do I make myself clear?'

From somewhere a long way off she heard herself say, 'As crystal.'

And somehow she found herself getting up from the table and going with him out into the night.

CHAPTER THREE

THE car he drove was new to her—low and sleek, with deep leather seats into which she sank almost helplessly. Music played softly, and she recognised that it was Bach—one of the Brandenburg concertos. It was all persuasively, beguilingly comfortable. And she was nearly, but not quite, lulled into acceptance...

She struggled to sit up straight. 'Where are we going?' she demanded huskily.

'To the hotel,' he said. 'Where else?'

'I'd prefer to go back to my own flat.'

'Which I'm sure has only a single bed,' Nick returned. 'We'll be marginally more comfortable at the Majestic, as I'm sure you'll appreciate.'

Cally drew a quick, angry breath. 'But you said—you promised... Oh, God, I should have known I couldn't trust you.'

'And I feel the same about you, darling. Did you really think I'd let you out of my sight?' He shook his head. 'No, Cally. You're spending the night with me. And, it's not lust, merely a safety precaution,' he added drily.

'But I have to go to the flat,' she protested. 'There are things I need—clothes and stuff.'

'If the clothing bears any resemblance to what you're wearing now, I suggest you leave it there,' he told her coolly. 'Besides, I've brought you everything you need. You once had a trousseau—remember?'

Cally smoothed the cheap material of her skirt over her knees in a defensive gesture. 'Yes—I remember.'

'You also had a wedding ring,' he went on. 'Is it still around?'

She stared through the windscreen into the night. 'I—threw it away.'

'How dramatic,' he said mockingly. 'Wiser to have sold it, perhaps. You must have needed the cash.'

But I wasn't feeling very wise. Just betrayed, confused and angry. The words trembled in her mind, but she did not utter them.

He said, 'I shall have to buy you another.'

She lifted her chin. 'Is that strictly necessary—for such a short time?'

'It's considered usual.'

'But I thought you weren't interested in conventions,' she said. 'Besides, I shall only throw it away again, when my duty's done and I claim my freedom.'

'However, while you're living as my wife you'll wear my ring.' His voice was soft, but there was a note in it that spelled danger. 'Just as you'll get used to sleeping in my bed. Who knows? You might even come to enjoy both of them.'

'Do not,' Cally said through gritted teeth, 'count on it.' She hesitated. 'How do you intend to explain my sudden return?'

'I don't,' Nick responded coolly. 'It concerns no one but ourselves.'

That, she thought, her nails curling into the palms of her hands, was not strictly true on a number of counts—not all of which she could bring herself to deal with. However, there was one she needed to mention.

She said tautly, 'I presume you've informed Adele—if she's still living at the Hall?'

'She isn't,' he said curtly. 'I arranged for her move to the Dower House months ago, when I still thought you might return of your own accord.'

She raised her brows. 'That can't have pleased her.'

'Nor did the prospect of finding herself replaced as the mistress of the house. Once I married, her departure became inevitable. She knew that.' He slanted a glance at her. 'Or did you wish to go on sharing a roof with her indefinitely?'

Her mouth tightened. 'No.'

'That's what I thought.' He sounded faintly amused. He turned the car under an archway and slotted it expertly into a cramped space in the small hotel car park. As they walked to the rear entrance Cally was conscious of his hand under her elbow.

When they reached the desk, she saw the blonde receptionist's eager smile take a disappointed downturn when she realised their most important guest was not alone.

Sorry, darling, but you never had a chance, Cally was tempted to tell her. He's already spoken for—and not by me.

Along with the key, she saw Nick accept a sheaf of messages, and then they were walking together to the lift.

As they rode up to the first floor she tried to think of something she could do or say that would let her off the hook for tonight at least. She wasn't ready, she thought desperately, for such a drastic change in her circumstances. She stole a look at her husband, but his dark face was expressionless.

The bridal suite consisted of a small, nondescript sitting room, with a writing desk and a television set, and a much larger bedroom containing a king-size bed with a white quilted satin coverlet sporting an enormous pink heart in its centre.

In spite of the nightmare scenario ahead of her, Cally knew an almost overwhelming desire to shriek with laughter. At the same time she found herself thinking that it was a far cry from the Virgin Islands, where their original honeymoon had been due to be spent. She tensed inwardly. She couldn't let herself think like that. Allow herself to remember a time when she'd been a naïve girl, wrapped up in her own fledgling dreams and hopes. Oblivious to the harsh truths of the world around her— even her small part of it...

'Your overnight case is there.' Nick's voice shocked her back to the present, and its realities, as he nodded towards the luggage stand. 'And the bathroom's through that door. I'll be in the sitting room, having a nightcap and dealing with my messages. It should take about twenty minutes.' He gave her a brief, formal smile. 'Can I get you anything?'

'No.' Her mouth was dry. *Twenty minutes*. 'Thank you.'

The door closed behind him, and Cally was alone. Temporarily at least.

She walked over to the bed and sank down on to the appalling cover, looking around her.

A resourceful person, she thought, should be able to escape from this situation—maybe by knotting sheets together and climbing out of a window. Except that a loud humming noise and frequent arctic blasts suggested that air-conditioning was in use and that the windows were hermetically sealed.

So it seemed she was committed beyond recall to this madness.

Her heart was fluttering against her ribs like a wounded bird, and her legs were shaking, but there was no point in staying where she was, with the minutes passing.

And there seemed little chance that Nick would agree to spend the night on the sofa in the sitting room, or allow her to do so. No matter how reluctant she might be, she would have to share this bed with him.

As for the future—her mind cringed away from its contemplation.

At least she knew now, with total certainty, why he'd asked her to marry him in the first place. Not because he'd ever wanted her in any real way, but because she was young, and probably fertile, and he needed her to give him a child. Something the woman he really loved could not provide, she thought, wincing as all the old pain and anger slashed at her again.

A year ago she'd been a naïve, trusting fool, but she would not fall into the same trap again. She'd accepted his terms now and she would adhere to them. There would be no more nonsense about imagining herself in love, or using Nick Tempest as the focus for her pathetic romantic fantasies. He was a businessman and he was offering her a business deal. Nothing more, nothing less.

She owed him, and he expected to be repaid. It was as simple as that.

And while she was with him she would learn to turn a blind eye to his extra-marital indiscretions. Steel herself never to ask where he was going, or where he had been. And, above all, never—ever—again follow him anywhere...

Those were matters of priority, and certainly she would be under no ludicrous illusions about love, marriage and 'happy ever after' this time around.

She got up and went across to the luggage stand, unzipping the overnight bag. The exquisite nightgown she'd bought with such shy hopes a year ago and never worn lay neatly folded on top of the other contents. She picked it up and shook it out, feeling the soft folds of white chiffon and lace drifting through her trembling fingers.

Everything in the case was new, in honour of her brand-new future, including the quilted apricot bag for toiletries with its pretty beaded embroidery. She took it, with the nightdress, into the bathroom.

The fittings were old-fashioned, and the shower was a trickle rather than a torrent, but she managed somehow, patting herself dry with one of the meagre towels. Then she slid the nightdress slowly over her head.

A year ago the chiffon would have enhanced slender, blossoming curves and made them seductive. Now it hung from her, she thought, giving herself a last disparaging glance in the mirror before turning away. Her shoulders and arms were thin, and her collarbones like pits. Her breasts were those of a child again.

But why should she repine? After all, the last thing in the world she wanted was for Nick to find her attractive. He liked beautiful women—he'd never made a secret of it. And for a while there, as she'd bloomed under his careful tutelage, she'd been—almost lovely.

But that girl no longer existed, and what was he left with instead? A rag, a bone, and a hank of hair. That was all.

And maybe the connoisseur in him, the sensualist, would not find that enough.

She trailed back into the other room, took clothes for the next day from the case—fresh underwear and a mid-calf dress in primrose linen, square-necked and cap-sleeved, which she hung up in one of the fitted wardrobes. After all, she'd bought it purposely to wear on the first day of the rest of her life, so it seemed an appropriate choice for tomorrow, if slightly sick.

And it was barely creased, indicating that her bag had not simply been left unopened and untouched over the past twelve months, as she'd thought likely.

Either that or she'd expected the entire contents of her luggage to have been removed to the nearest charity shop, erasing all physical reminders of her from his life. And yet it was all still there, wrapped in tissue and waiting for her.

He really had intended that she should go back to him, she thought shivering.

Her time was nearly up, so, with another apprehensive glance towards the sitting room, she reluctantly climbed into the wide bed, hugging its extreme edge as she reached up and turned off the pink-shaded befrilled lamp. Lying rigidly on her side, she closed her eyes tightly and kept them closed, trying to breathe deeply and evenly as if she was asleep.

It seemed an eternity before the door between them opened quietly and she knew she was no longer alone. She was aware of Nick moving about softly, then the click of the bathroom door, and beyond it the noise from the shower.

Cally tried to relax—to sink down into the mattress—giving the impression that she was dead to the world. But it wasn't easy—not with tension building inside her all the while.

For the first time in her life she was about to spend a night in bed with a man, and in spite of his assurances she was petrified.

Eventually she heard him come back into the room and walk

quietly across to the bed. There was a soft rustle like silk, as if he was removing a dressing gown, then she felt the mattress dip slightly as he joined her. The other equally awful pink lamp was extinguished, and the room was dark.

He was nowhere near Cally, maintaining his distance as promised, but she was intensely conscious of his presence just the same. His skin smelt cool and fresh with the fragrance of soap, and some unguessed-at female instinct told her, without a shadow of a doubt, that he was naked.

She froze. Her heart was thudding like a trapped animal beating against the bars of its cage as she waited tensely.

'For God's sake, relax.' His voice in the heavy darkness was weary with exasperation. 'I don't go in for force.'

At least not tonight, Cally thought, but did not dare say it.

'Can't you understand how difficult this is for me?' she demanded tautly.

'I don't find the situation easy either,' Nick retorted sharply. 'But we have to start our marriage somewhere, and tradition suggests that bed is the place.'

'For lovers, perhaps.' Her riposte was more acerbic than she'd intended. There was a silence.

Then he asked gently, 'Is that intended as some kind of challenge?'

Cally found her eyes were so tightly closed that coloured spots danced behind her lids. 'No,' she mumbled.

'Good,' he said. 'Let's keep it that way, shall we?' He paused again. 'And bed isn't simply about sex, Cally. It's also a quiet and private place to talk sometimes.'

'You're implying we have something to discuss? So far you've simply issued instructions.'

'I thought you might wish to go into a little more detail about why you ran away from me.'

Cally's eyes flew open. She hunched a shoulder. 'It seemed like a good idea at the time. As it happens, it still does.'

'And that's your final word on the subject?' He sounded more curious than angry.

'At the moment,' she said, 'my most pressing concern is the future—not the past.'

'Really?' he said. 'And I thought it was the here and now that had you clinging to the edge of the bed like an abseiler whose rope has been cut.'

'If so, you can hardly blame me for that.'

'You were the one who asked for a breathing space,' Nick reminded her softly.

At this particular time it seemed difficult to breathe at all, Cally realised, her throat tightening.

She said huskily, 'You can hardly expect to—walk back into my life and expect things to be as they were a year ago.'

'Ah,' he said. 'And exactly how were things then, Cally? Refresh my memory.'

Oh, God, she'd walked bang into that one, she thought, biting her lip.

She steadied her voice. 'Perhaps I believed—once—briefly—that a marriage between us could be made to work.'

'And yet you walked out?' he said slowly. 'Without even a shot being fired in anger. Why? And I want a reason. Not some flippant throwaway excuse that tells me nothing.'

It was the direct question she'd dreaded, and it demanded the direct answer she could not give.

Because I discovered I'd been blind enough and crazy enough to give you the power to smash me into little pieces. To break my heart so cruelly and completely that I would never recover.

Because it was only when I saw you with another woman in your arms on our wedding day that I realised how deeply I'd fallen in love with you, and that it would kill me to live only half a life with you—knowing that I would have to share you. That it was her that you really wanted—not me—and ours was just a marriage of convenience.

Knowing, too, that any happiness I found would be a sham and a betrayal.

And that the only way I could retain my sanity—and my self-

respect—would be to distance myself from you totally, utterly and for ever.

But to say the words aloud would be another fatal betrayal. She would be admitting that his pretence at wooing her had succeeded only too well, and that as she'd stood beside him and repeated her vows she'd been loving and longing for him with shy but passionate ardour.

And to let him know that she'd been such a pathetic, gullible fool was more than flesh and blood could stand. She could not bear such a stark humiliation.

Better, she thought, to endure Nick's anger than his pity.

She had no idea, of course, if Vanessa Layton was still part of his life. If she was even now installed at Southwood Cottage, or whether she'd been supplanted by someone else.

No doubt she would find out soon enough, she told herself, her whole being wincing from the thought. But what she must never do was give Nick even a hint that she cared. That his blatant disregard for fidelity mattered to her so badly that seeing him with Vanessa had torn her apart, leaving her torn and bleeding. And running away, like a small wounded animal seeking sanctuary, had seemed the only possible remedy. A chance to heal herself somehow—eventually.

As he'd admitted himself, he was not and never had been the marrying kind. But he needed someone to run his home efficiently—and, it now seemed, to give him a child. With Nick there was always an agenda.

And I was conveniently available, she thought, and so pitifully ready to believe every charming, seductive lie he told me. Not to mention the merit points he'd gain by rescuing the neighbourhood's penniless orphan. Why couldn't I see that he was taking me in lieu of the money my grandfather owed him? That was why he could still justify continuing his affair with Vanessa—because he was just balancing the bloody books.

She drew a ragged, painful breath.

He said harshly, 'I'm waiting for an answer.'

Slowly, reluctantly, she turned to face him. Her eyes were

accustomed now to the semi-darkness, and she could see that he was propped up on one elbow, watching her, although she was unable to read his expression. But then, did she really want to?

She said, 'I told you—I knew I'd made a terrible mistake and I couldn't think how to put it right. So I suppose I took the coward's way out—and left.'

'And that's all there was to it?'

'Yes.' *Or all she could ever admit to.*

'It didn't occur to you to talk to me? That maybe together we could have sorted something out?'

'I was afraid that—somehow—you'd persuade me to stay.' That, she thought, at least was the truth.

'It's almost comforting to know that once seemed possible.' His tone was wry.

'I can assure you it didn't last long,' she said defensively.

'Now, that carries real conviction,' he returned grimly. 'But if that's a way of telling me I still have a struggle on my hands, I recommend that you think again. Because I've no intention of fighting fair.'

She said tonelessly, 'I'll consider myself warned.'

'On the other hand,' he said, after a pause, 'it doesn't have to be like this.'

'As long as I do what you say? Play by your rules?' Cally demanded bitterly. 'Oh, I'm sure.'

'I was thinking more,' Nick said slowly, 'of that day by the river. And please don't pretend you've forgotten.'

Her instinctive denial died on her lips. She tensed. 'What of it?'

'It would be good,' he said, 'if we could forget the rest and recapture that time—that place.'

He made a slight movement, adjusting his position, and she felt him touch her shoulder, quietly and softly, his fingers cool as drops of water against the sudden burn of her naked skin.

A fist seemed to clench in her chest as reluctantly, painfully, she found herself remembering…

Reliving in too-vivid detail the nearby whisper of running water, the scent of the grass, and the glow of the sun against her closed eyelids. And Nick's mouth on hers, gentling her lips apart, bringing her to trembling life with the delicate play of his tongue against hers and the slow, beguiling drift of his fingers on her body.

While, deep within her, she'd felt the first bewildering, tormenting ache of desire—overwhelming and irresistible.

It might have been yesterday. It could be now...

Now! The word seemed to sting her brain, sending her crashing back to sanity. Oh, God, she groaned silently, what was she thinking of?

Gasping in shock, she jerked away from him. 'Don't—don't touch me. I—I can't bear it.'

There was a silence, then he spoke, his voice soft and jeering. 'What are you hoping, my sweet? That you'll offend me so deeply I'll toss you back to your good Samaritan at Gunners Wharf and crawl away, wounded, into the undergrowth?' He shook his head. 'You'll have to try harder than that, darling. And I think it's time to give some thought to the actual terms of our agreement,' he added with a touch of grimness. 'Because, under the circumstances, a little touching is going to be inevitable.'

Her mouth was dry. 'But not yet. Not so soon—please.'

'A pleasure deferred, then,' Nick drawled mockingly.

She winced. 'How can you possibly say that?'

'Easily,' he said. 'Because I intend to enjoy every inch of you—and every moment of our time together.' He paused. 'You, of course, must do as you please.' He reached out an arm and flicked on the lamp at his side of the bed, bathing the room in pink light.

Cally stiffened. 'What are you doing?'

He said quietly, 'If I'm not allowed to touch, I may at least look.' He took the edge of the covers and tossed them back.

Cally made an unavailing grab for their protection, then lay like a stone, staring into space, her lower lip caught in her teeth, bitterly aware that the delicate layer of chiffon was no barrier at all against his cool, lingering scrutiny of her body.

At last, she said in a small, stifled voice, 'Have you finished?'

He gave a brief, harsh laugh. 'Don't be naïve, darling. We both know I haven't even begun yet.'

He turned away from her, onto his side, extinguishing the light and leaving her to draw the covers back into place. She lay beside him, imprisoned by silence and his proximity, not daring to move.

Even when his quiet, steady breathing told her that he was asleep, Cally could not relax. How could he be so casual—so unfazed, she asked herself, when he was behaving so abominably?

He'd meant everything he said, she thought, fear tightening her throat. They had a bargain, and—sooner or later—she would be made to keep her side of it.

How many women did he want in his life at any given time? she wondered, almost hysterically. And what kind of man made time for his mistress just before he was due to depart on honeymoon with his brand-new bride?

The cynicism of that terrified her.

But even if she confronted him about it—accused him, told him openly that was why she'd left, why she could not bring herself to live with him as his wife—would it make any real difference? He'd simply shrug it off, without guilt or remorse. A deal that had not paid off.

Or, even worse, he might see it as a confession of weakness on her part. A sign that she cared more then she'd ever been prepared to admit.

And she couldn't risk that. Not at this juncture.

Cally brought her clenched fist up to her mouth, sinking her teeth into the knuckles.

Her disappearance had undoubtedly embarrassed him, and it would certainly anger him if she reneged on their bargain a second time. But Nick wouldn't suffer—not as she'd done a year ago, she thought with anguish. Or as the Gunners Wharf residents would when he pulled the plug on their housing scheme. As he assuredly would.

And she would be left to endure the guilt of that—knowing that she could have prevented it if she'd submitted to his demands.

But the reality of what he was asking had settled on her like a stone, and she felt crushed by its weight.

A baby, she thought. A tiny human being to be created and carried in her womb. To be brought into the world for her to love and nurture. Or, as seemed more likely, a prize to be fought over by two warring strangers.

Cally shivered. That wasn't what she wanted. How could it be? Yet he'd already set off an emotional alarm bell. 'Joint custody,' he'd said. 'At first anyway.'

Those were the words that had set off reverberations in her mind. That lingered.

Indicating—what, exactly? That there might come a time when she'd be expected to surrender her rights to her own child? Virtually give up her baby for adoption by a man rich enough to pay for his slightest wish to be fulfilled, and sufficiently powerful to fight anyone who stood in his way?

Was Nick really capable of being that uncaring—that ruthless? Or would he simply say that the end—somehow—justified the means, and believe it?

Oh, dear God, she thought achingly. Please—please don't let it be so.

Yet he'd told her frankly that marriage wasn't for him. That once she'd fulfilled his terms she'd be free to leave. But he hadn't mentioned the baby.

If, of course, there was a baby…

She'd always assumed that one day she'd be a mother. After all, it was the next natural progression from being a wife. But, like so much in their relationship, she and Nick had never actually discussed the possibility.

And it had certainly never occurred to her that he regarded her as some kind of brood mare.

Her pregnancy, she thought wretchedly, should have been one of the crowning moments of their love. Except that the love had never existed, and now one of the supreme joys of a woman's life was being reduced to the status of duty. Transformed into an obligation.

For the past year she had been alone. But in the next months she seemed fated to learn the true nature of loneliness itself.

And how could she bear it?

Cally slept at last, exhausted by the weary treadmill of her thoughts.

When she awoke, she lay for a moment, feeling disorientated, wondering where she was. Then memory prompted her, and she turned her head slowly, looking with trepidation at the bed beside her. But it was empty, only the rumpled pillows and the covers tossed back revealing that the space had ever been occupied.

And, as if on some silent cue, Nick emerged from the bathroom, immaculately shaved, dark hair still damp, fastening links into the cuffs of his shirt.

'Good morning.' His tone was brisk. 'The bathroom's all yours, and I've ordered breakfast in fifteen minutes, so I suggest you get a move on. We have things to do, and I want to be back at Wylstone by early afternoon.'

'You're planning to return there today—taking me with you?' Cally was astounded.

'Naturally.' His brows lifted. 'Just as soon as the Gunners Terrace business is completed.'

'But you have to give me some leeway here,' she protested huskily. 'You can't expect me simply to—abandon everything and leave.'

He said icily, 'I didn't expect it last time, sweetheart, but you managed it all the same. And you've had a year of ducking and weaving since then to perfect your technique.' He paused, allowing that to sink in, then added, 'Now, get dressed—unless you want me to help you?'

'No.' She bit her lip. 'I can manage.'

The shower seemed to be working better this morning. Nick had probably given it an executive order, she thought rebelliously, as she zipped herself into the yellow dress, ran a cursory brush through her hair, and went to join him in the other room.

A trolley had just been brought in, and Cally saw grapefruit, croissants with dishes of butter and preserves, and a tall pot of coffee.

Nick rose. 'Come and sit down,' he said, indicating the sofa beside him, and she reluctantly complied.

He put a hand under her chin, surveying her critically. 'I have to say that you don't look particularly rested.'

'I hardly slept at all,' Cally said curtly, jerking her head away. 'I'm not used to sharing a bed—particularly with a man.'

His mouth twisted sardonically. 'Just one of many new experiences waiting for you, darling.'

She said slowly, 'I hoped—I prayed—that when I woke up this morning it would all be just a bad dream. Or a cruel joke.' She swallowed. 'Nick—please tell me that's all it was. Say that you didn't mean any of the things you said last night. Because I—I think I've been punished enough.'

'It's straightforward enough,' he said, pouring the coffee. 'And I meant every word. Give me a child, and in return you'll get your divorce. What part of that do you not understand?'

She said in a low voice, 'I can't understand how you can bear to do this to me. It's barbaric.'

'Your own behaviour, of course, being so civilised,' Nick returned mockingly. 'Have some coffee, and spare us the cliché of saying it would choke you.'

Those very words had been on the tip of Cally's tongue, but, chagrined, she bit them back, and accepted the cup he held out to her in smouldering silence.

The coffee was surprisingly good, black and strong, putting

heart into her and enabling her to say eventually, 'When we reach Wylstone I'd like to move back into the courtyard flat—at first, anyway.'

'I'm afraid that won't be possible.' Nick said without the least sign of regret as he finished his grapefruit and put down the spoon. 'I'd have to evict the Thurstons, and they wouldn't be happy about it.'

Cally frowned. 'The Thurstons?'

'The couple who work for me.' He chose a croissant from the dish.

'What happened to Mrs Bridges?' She was astounded. Sir Ranald's housekeeper had been there for years—almost part of the fabric of the building.

His mouth quirked in faint amusement. 'She preferred to follow Adele into exile. But the Thurstons are a terrific find. You'll like them.'

'I doubt that.' Mutinously, she returned her cup to the trolley.

'Then at least try not to show your dislike too obviously,' he said silkily. 'Save it for me instead, or I'll have to raise their salaries.' He paused. 'Are you going to eat something?'

'I'm not hungry.'

His brows lifted. 'Planning to starve yourself into an early grave? Or simply become anorexic?'

'Neither,' she said curtly. 'I'm not a breakfast person.'

'I stand corrected.' This time the glance he sent her was openly amused. 'But maybe you should change your ways, darling. After all, you need to keep your strength up.'

'I imagine I'm strong enough for your purposes.' Cally lifted her chin.

'Ouch,' Nick said with perfect amiability, and went on eating his croissant.

Oh, God, he was so pleased with himself—so enjoying his triumph, thought Cally, her hands clenching in the folds of her skirt.

She took a deep breath. 'If it can't be the flat, then maybe there's somewhere else I can have. For a while. Somewhere of my own. Some space.' She swallowed. 'One room would do.'

'You'll have the whole house,' he said. 'During the day, at least. The nights, of course, will be a different matter.' He got to his feet, dusting his fingers briskly with his napkin, then dropping it on to the trolley. 'And now it's time we were going.'

Cally rose too. She said bitterly, 'You're not prepared to make any concessions, are you?'

Nick picked up his jacket. He said quietly, 'I gave you last night. But today our marriage begins.' He paused. 'So, shall we go down to Gunners Wharf with the good news? I'll let you break it to them, darling. Credit where credit is due, after all.'

Her stormy gaze met the icy mockery in his.

She said, quietly but clearly, 'Damn you to hell, Nick Tempest.' Then, head high, she walked back into the bedroom to get her bag.

CHAPTER FOUR

'YOU look so different,' Kit said. 'I've never seen you in anything but black, white and grey. Now suddenly you're in Technicolor.' He surveyed her moodily. 'You look—amazing. But I feel as if I've never known you at all.'

Cally stifled a sigh. 'I didn't intend that you should,' she said quietly. 'Because I wasn't planning to stay. And I'm just here to clear my desk,' she added. 'Not part bad friends.'

'And I had no idea your name was Caroline until Tempest said it,' he went on, as if she hadn't spoken. 'Why did you call yourself Cally?'

She shrugged defensively. 'When I was learning to talk, that was all of Caroline I could manage. It—stuck.'

He shook his head. 'No wonder I never stood a chance. He's a rich man, isn't he? A multimillionaire.' There was a note of self-pity in his voice that jarred on her. 'And you've let him buy you.'

Have I? Cally thought. Then, if so, why am I paying the price?

Aloud, she said wearily, 'Kit—let's not over-dramatise the situation. I'm going back to my husband—that's all. It was bound to happen sooner or later.' *At least that's what I have to believe.* She paused. 'And please remember I offered you nothing.'

'No,' Kit said bitterly. 'I'm not likely to forget that.'

Cally slammed the empty drawer shut. 'Also, you seem to be overlooking the fact that Gunners Terrace is alive and well,' she said crisply. 'We just happen to have won a famous victory, and Leila, Tracy and the others are jumping for joy out there. You should be over the moon for them too, joining in the celebrations.'

'Well, perhaps I'm not in a celebratory mood,' he snapped back, just as Nick appeared in the doorway, glancing expressionlessly between Kit's wrathful flush and Cally's taut self-containment.

'Finished up here, darling?' he asked pleasantly. 'Because it's time we were leaving.' He walked over to her, sliding an arm round her body, his hand resting on the curve of her slender hip in a gesture of total possession.

Cally saw Kit register the gesture, then turn away sullenly.

'Yes,' she said. 'I'm—ready.'

There hadn't been much to collect. A few pens, a picture one of the children had painted for her, and a paperweight that Mrs Hartley had given her when Cally had inadvertently revealed it was her birthday the previous day. It was a lovely thing, in shades of azure and emerald flecked with gold, like a dive into a sunlit tropical sea, and she could not have left it behind. She'd brought nothing at all from the flat, which would be cleared out by the landlord—whose protests Nick had silenced with a month's rent in lieu of notice.

Money really seemed to be the answer to everything, she thought bitterly.

One by one, her tenuous ties to this place had been cut. Now nothing remained but her future with Nick, and that was only temporary.

Her whole life had suddenly become a leap into the dark.

She said quietly, 'Goodbye, Kit. I hope the whole project goes from strength to strength.'

'Thank you.' He did not look at her.

For a moment she wanted to scream at him. Do you know— do you have any idea what I've done? The sacrifice I've had to make?

But that would imply his attitude was justified, that she owed him some kind of explanation. Whereas she knew she didn't, and it was best to let the matter drop—walk away. With her husband's arm holding her like a ring of steel. Staking his claim.

As they reached the main door, she said tautly, 'Why don't you just give me a label to wear—''Nick's Woman''?'

'I thought I had.' His tone was clipped. 'In St John's church, twelve months ago.'

Cally winced, but could think of nothing to say in reply.

Everyone was waiting outside the Centre to see them leave, and the euphoria was almost tangible.

Tracy came rushing up and enveloped her in a hug. 'You don't look as if you slept much last night, you lucky girl,' she whispered with a giggle. 'Be happy. And don't forget us.'

There was a terrible irony in that, thought Cally, forcing a smile and nodding.

'Come along, darling.' Nick drew her close to his side again, his fingers laced with hers in a parody of intimacy as they walked to the car. He turned to give a last smile—a wave. Like visiting royalty, she thought, swallowing back the bubble of hysteria that was threatening to overwhelm her.

It was almost a relief to find herself inside the car and driving away from it all.

I should have done that a long time ago, she thought broodingly. Instead of hanging around, waiting tamely to be found. And now it's all too late...

'Will you miss Wellingford?' Nick's tone was casual.

'No,' she said. 'I never planned to stay. Especially after Mrs Hartley died. She was a terrific lady.'

'But not particularly blessed in her sons,' he commented ironically.

She shrugged. 'Perhaps they take after their father,' she said, adding pointedly, 'It can happen.'

And heard him laugh softly.

They were soon on the motorway, the big car comfortably eating up the miles, transporting Cally swiftly and silently to her new life and all that it implied.

Although it seemed she would at least be miserable in luxury, she told herself wryly. The car was air-conditioned, its windows tinted to diffuse the brightness of the sunlight.

And Nick was a good driver, she was forced to admit, stealing a sideways glance at him from beneath her lashes. She'd never before accompanied him on a long journey, and had expected their progress to be aggressively conducted, with him cutting a triumphal swathe through the traffic. But she was wrong. He handled his beautiful vehicle with sure skill, driving fast but safely, with surprising tolerance for the vagaries of his fellow motorists.

He'd discarded his jacket and loosened his tie, and his shirt-sleeves were rolled back to reveal tanned forearms.

He looked totally relaxed—even as if he was enjoying himself, she thought, biting at her lower lip.

He asked if she wanted music and she agreed, simply because it was preferable to conversation—especially if he had questions she'd no wish to answer. But he seemed to prefer to concentrate on the road, rather than be diverted by contentious issues.

She was aware of the music, a smooth blues combo, but she wasn't listening to it. She couldn't. Not when every mile was taking her nearer to Wylstone, and the associations of misery and humiliation that haunted it. Memories that she would be forced to endure, along with so much else, she thought, swallowing convulsively.

She'd tried to use the last twelve months to wrench them out of her brain and dismiss them for ever. She'd thought she'd succeeded. That she'd cured herself of the virus that was Nick Tempest. Yet she'd only had to see him again and they were all back, clamouring obscenely for her attention.

Telling her that all she'd really done was use a sticking plaster to cover a mortal wound.

How could this have happened to me? she asked herself numbly. Was there nothing—*nothing* that I could have done?

But she already knew the answer to that. The path of her life seemed to have led her straight to him.

Even the impulse that had caused her to absent herself to London safely out of Nick's orbit, had been cancelled out by the breakdown in her grandfather's health that had summoned her back so arbitrarily.

I was all my grandfather had, she thought wearily. So what choice did I have—then or ever?

And then, with frightening suddenness, her life had begun to fall apart. Inevitably, Nick had been there with his safety net, offering her grandfather and herself a home and a kind of security. It had been the perfect opportunity for him, she thought. Everything had conspired to bring them together, and he had placed her under the kind of obligation that could only have one ending.

She should have realised that one day some kind of recompense would be demanded from her—if not in cash, because there wasn't any, then certainly in kind. She should have known that Nick had marked her out from the start as his future bride—young, she thought stormily, and biddable. Not a living, feeling girl, but a puppet, easy to manipulate. Or so he'd considered. And she, pitifully, had totally misread his intentions.

Well, at least she'd forced him to think again. To accept that she wasn't the naïve push-over he'd originally bargained for. Ready to sacrifice her emotions, her self-respect and her trust in exchange for a roof over her head and his money to spend.

Except that it had not been about money at all. And the knowledge of that had provided the basis for the private tragedy that was beginning to unfold.

'I suppose you know that you're trespassing?' Those were the first words Nick had ever said to her, and she would never forget them.

In a way, it had been a covert warning that he was forbidden territory and she encroached there at her peril. And she'd picked up on it, even if it was at some unconscious level. Wasn't that why she'd taken the job in London—in order to put distance between them and recover from the threat to her untried emotional equilibrium?

But where Nick was concerned her instincts had always been heightened, she recognised. Hence the bad dreams over the past year, signalling to her that his net had been spread again. That the search was on in earnest.

I should have listened, she thought. Found another country to live in, even.

Except, of course, that her passport had been left in her hand luggage back at Wylstone Hall, ready for the honeymoon that never was. Stranding her in Britain, within his reach. A mistake she would not make again once she was finally free.

She became aware that they were pulling off the motorway, traversing a roundabout into a smaller country road.

She sat up. 'Where are we going?'

'There's a good pub not far away,' he said. 'And you need food.' She was aware of his swift, sideways glance. 'Or are you going to tell me you're not a lunch person either?'

Actually, she was ravenous, but she wasn't about to admit it.

She lifted her chin. 'Just as you wish.'

'If only it were that simple,' he murmured with faint amusement.

They drew up a short while afterwards outside an old-fashioned country inn, an ancient timbered building with low ceilings and uneven floors, and, at the rear, well-kept gardens, bright with flowers, and a lawn stretching down to the river, offering tables shaded by parasols.

'Will this do?' Nick halted at a table in an arbour, heavy with climbing roses just coming into flower.

'Fine.' Cally picked up a menu and hid behind it.

'They're famous here for their pies.' Nick seated himself opposite. 'I'm ordering steak and kidney. How about you?'

Cally, who had no wish to enter into the spirit of the occasion, tried to work up an interest in the sandwich list, and failed utterly. 'Turkey and ham,' she capitulated, after a brief struggle. 'And a glass of dry white wine—please.'

She watched him cross the grass to deliver their order, and saw how women's heads turned as if operated by strings when he passed by. Two pretty girls at an adjoining table were waiting, saucer-eyed, for his return.

And it was worth waiting for. Even she had to acknowledge that. In a crowd of thousands, she would still be able to pick out that long, lithe stride. Feel the pull of that cool, understated masculinity, and the unwelcome stir of her own senses in response.

To her embarrassment, he saw her watching his approach and smiled across at her. She looked away, swiftly and blindly.

As he put down the drinks and resumed his seat Cally said, quietly and urgently, 'Nick, it's still not too late. We don't have to do this.'

His brows lifted. 'You want to change your order? Or go somewhere else? I thought you'd like it here.'

Her voice shook slightly. 'That's not what I meant, and you know it.'

His mouth twisted. 'Well—perhaps,' he conceded drily. 'So, what exactly are you saying?'

Cally lifted her chin, 'That if you announced you were looking for a surrogate mother for your baby the queue would form on the right. Because that's all you really want—isn't it? You—you don't need to involve me.'

'Oh, yes, I do, darling,' he said softly. 'And that's why I'm not going for surrogacy, or adoption, or even down the IVF route, or any other potential means of escape that fertile brain of yours can summon up.' His smile was hard—implacable. 'You married me, Cally, for better or worse. And now, a little belatedly, you're going to learn to be my wife.' He added harshly, 'The number of lessons required will depend entirely on yourself.'

Her breath caught. She said huskily, 'You—really want your pound of flesh, don't you?'

The grey eyes narrowed as they studied her, lingering with explicit appreciation on the deep neckline of the yellow dress, the way its fabric clung to her small high breasts.

He said quietly, 'I want all of you, Caroline. No protests and nothing held back. And no less will do.'

She swallowed. 'I—think I just lost my appetite.'

'Unfortunate,' he said. 'Then you'll just have to watch me eat instead.' He paused. 'Tell me something, Cally. Is it the whole idea of sex that repels you, or merely the thought of having it with me?'

She stared down at the table. 'I ran away from you,' she said, expressionlessly. 'I'd have thought that made my feelings clear.'

'No, darling,' he said. 'Now, as always, your emotions remain an enigma.' He lifted his beer glass mockingly. 'To marriage,' he said, and drank.

In spite of her previous disavowal, Cally found that lunch, when it came, was irresistible. The pies arrived, golden-brown in individual earthenware pots, accompanied by dishes of vegetables, and were served by the waitresses onto their plates. As the crusts broke, spilling their fragrant contents across the porcelain, the aroma literally made her mouth water.

There was no way she could refuse to eat. Nor would she achieve anything by starving herself, she admitted resignedly.

She was expecting a sarcastic comment from Nick as she reached for her cutlery, but he only permitted himself a swift, ironic glance before applying himself to his own food.

'Dessert?' he asked, when she finally put down her knife and fork.

She said stiltedly, 'Just coffee, please. Black, no sugar.'

'I'll have the same.' Nick offered a brief smile to the girl who'd come to clear their plates, then bent to help retrieve the cutlery she'd instantly and blushingly dropped on the grass.

'Poor girl,' Cally commented as the waitress retreated. 'You seem to have a devastating effect on women.'

'Not often,' Nick returned silkily. 'And certainly not on you, my sweet.'

Ah, but that's not true, she thought. Or how did you so easily persuade me to marry you—against all my better judgement? I wasn't proof against your smile either—or the way you looked at me. Or the kisses and caresses that always left me aching for more.

'You're attracting a lot of attention yourself,' Nick added, breaking into her reverie. 'But that's hardly surprising. In that dress, you look like part of the sunlight.'

Cally flushed and looked away self-consciously from the sudden intensity of his gaze. 'Please—don't say things like that.'

'I'm not even allowed to pay you a mild compliment?'

'Not,' she said, 'in our kind of bargain.'

'Yet it's no more than the truth,' Nick said. 'Just look around you if you don't believe me.'

She said tautly, 'If people are staring, it's only to wonder what the hell someone like me is doing with someone like you, and we both know it.'

'I know nothing of the kind.' There was a new harshness in his tone. 'Why do you constantly denigrate yourself, Cally?'

'I think they actually call it being aware of one's limitations,' she said. 'I learned it quite early in life.'

'From your grandfather, I suppose,' he said with faint grimness.

'You can hardly blame him.' She shrugged. 'After all, he didn't have the grandson he'd set his heart on, so the next best thing was a replica of the daughter he'd lost—someone beautiful, vibrant and glamorous, with real star appeal. I—fell a long way short of his expectations.'

He said, slowly, 'My God.'

'It's understandable.' She took a breath. 'My mother was—a very hard act to follow. She and my father worshipped each other. In a way, it was a blessing the accident took them both, because they'd never have survived alone.'

'They wouldn't have been alone.' His voice was very quiet. 'They had you.'

'As it was, I was left with Grandfather. In the aftermath of it all we were both grieving, but we couldn't seem to comfort each other. Still, I think—eventually—he came to love me—in his way.' She paused. 'And he wanted me to be looked after when he'd gone. To have the financial security that he hadn't been able to provide himself at the end.' Her voice faltered slightly.

'Which, of course, is where I came in.' Nick ironically supplied her unspoken words.

'Grandfather's final act.' She forced a smile. 'To arrange my future. Hand me one of the glittering prizes. He even managed to make me believe, for a while, that it was what I wanted too.'

'And then Cinderella tried on the slipper and found it was the wrong size,' he said softly. 'Poor Cally.'

'What does it matter?' she said. 'I won't be wearing it for long. So there's really no need to pity me. Whatever you force me to do, I'll survive.'

She turned deliberately in her chair and stared at the river. Its still waters were golden-green in the brightness, shading to oily darkness in the overhang of the willows that fringed it. A small group of ducks was quarrelling noisily over the bread some diners had thrown for them, and from the opposite bank a diminutive but stately moorhen emerged from the reeds, her brood of chicks strung out behind her, all paddling frantically to keep up.

In spite of herself, Cally found some of the tension seeping out of her, her lips curving with pleasure.

She said, half to herself, 'It's just so beautiful here.'

'Would you like to stay the night?' Nick asked quietly. 'They have rooms, and it's early in the season, so there are probably vacancies.' His smile touched her skin, warming it in spite of herself. 'We could have a mini-honeymoon.'

Cally stiffened, her heart thudding. 'No,' she stated with cool clarity. 'I don't want to stay. Thank you.'

'As you wish,' he said equably. 'I just wanted to demonstrate that force isn't an essential element of our time together.'

There was an odd silence that Cally hastened to fill. 'Anyway, I thought you were desperate to get back to Wylstone.'

'Not that desperate,' he said softly. 'After all, my love, you seem to have an affinity with the banks of rivers that might be worth exploiting.'

Her flush deepened. 'An isolated incident,' she said grittily, 'that I'd prefer to forget.'

'And one of my most treasured memories,' he murmured. 'I've often thought since that I should have taken you then—when I had the chance.'

Cally sent him a fulminating glance, and was relieved to turn her attention to the arrival of their coffee.

As she filled their cups from the cafetière, she said stiltedly, 'Is your mother well?'

'According to her last letter, she's bursting with health,' Nick returned drily. 'She's also planning to pay us a visit.'

Cally digested this piece of news uneasily as she passed Nick his coffee. She had never met Cecily Tempest, who was a distinguished archaeologist, whose working life was concentrated in the jungles of Central America. She'd thought that she never would.

She said, 'I thought she was in Guatemala.'

'It seems the present excavations need a new injection of funding. She's coming back to do a series of lectures, and raise some more cash.' He paused. 'And, at some point, meet her new daughter-in-law.'

'I see,' Cally said slowly. 'Yet another reason for you to need my urgent return.' She swallowed some hot coffee. 'Have you told her that we've been living apart?'

'I decided against that. After all, I'd only just told her that we were getting married. The news that I was a bachelor again so soon might have aroused her latent maternal instinct and brought her hurrying home to investigate, so I thought it best not to burden her.'

'Of course.' Her voice was tight. 'And now there's no necessity for embarrassing explanations. Because I'm back.' She paused. 'I presume I'm required to play the part of the loving and dutiful wife?'

'I certainly hope so,' he said silkily. 'But she's not arriving immediately, so you'll have plenty of time to rehearse. And you'll need it. When it comes to digging, my mother isn't solely interested in Mayan artefacts.'

Cally bit her lip. 'You certainly have everything worked out in advance.'

'If I had,' Nick said tersely, 'I would not have spent my wedding night alone last year.'

'I've only your word for it that you did,' Cally fired back

without thinking, and paused, appalled at her own indiscretion. Remembering too late that she'd forbidden herself any reference to Nick's infidelity with Vanessa Layton.

Oh, God, she groaned inwardly. I've just broken my own taboo. Now he's going to ask what I mean—and I don't know what to say. How to find an explanation that doesn't make me sound like some pathetic, jealous idiot.

'Are you crazy?' The grey eyes were like steel. 'My attention was fully occupied in looking for you, darling, not choosing a substitute bedmate. Besides, you're going to atone fully for any previous disappointment you caused me,' he added harshly.

Cally drank the rest of her coffee and put down the cup. She said, 'I—really don't need any further reminders.'

His smile was as hard as his gaze. 'In that case, shall we be leaving?'

As he pushed back his chair and rose she said bitterly, 'And let's not pretend I have a choice.'

She was aware of the envious glances following her as she walked at his side back to the inn to pay the bill.

She thought If you knew—if you only knew... And could have wept.

They travelled in silence. Cally sat with her hands folded in her lap, staring sightlessly through the windscreen, her thoughts caught on the same weary treadmill.

The car was her cage. The motorway her path to her own personal hell. And there was nothing more she could do. No argument—no appeal she could offer—carried any weight with him, as he'd made mockingly clear from the beginning.

Nick had bought her, and now he expected to see a return on his investment—however temporary.

She leaned back in her seat, closing her eyes, listening to the smooth hum of the motor, images from the past dissolving and reforming as the edges of her consciousness started to blur.

'I suppose you know that you're trespassing?'

And her own reply, made defensive by guilt, as she stared down from the back of her horse at the tall young man con-

fronting her on the path. 'I was just taking a shortcut across the edge of the wood. Sir Ranald never objected.'

'Unfortunately Sir Ranald's no longer around to express an opinion either way,' he said. 'But I am, and I came out after pigeon.' He indicated the gun he was carrying. 'Supposing I'd accidentally winged you instead? Or your horse? In future, sweetheart, take the long way round.' The strange silver-grey eyes flickered over her, absorbing the damp cotton shirt outlining her small breasts, her slender denim-clad thighs. He added quietly, 'You'll find it safer.'

And with another long, considering look he turned and vanished as abruptly as he'd appeared, leaving Cally to lean forward on Baz's neck, gasping as if she'd been winded after a gallop, instead of merely taking a gentle hack across someone else's land as she'd done so often before.

But never again, she swore as she clicked her tongue to Baz and they set off again. In future she'd give the Wylstone estate, and its new owner, a very wide berth.

And she'd meant it, Cally thought. From then on she'd scrupulously avoided any diversions through the dappled shade of the Home Wood.

And then she'd come in from shopping one day to find her grandfather entertaining a visitor in the drawing room.

'Ah, come in, my dear,' Robert Naylor had hailed her. 'Tempest, I don't think you've met my granddaughter, Caroline. Cally—this is poor Ranald's cousin, Sir Nicholas Tempest. He plans to live at Wylstone, so the rumours were wrong. We're going to have neighbours after all.'

'No, we haven't been formally introduced.' Nicholas Tempest's mouth was solemn as he shook hands with her, but the grey eyes were sparking with amusement. 'I came to ask your grandfather to dine with me next week,' he went on, his fingers still holding hers. 'I hope you'll be able to accompany him.'

'Of course she will,' Robert said robustly. 'She must find life damned slow down here, spending her time with an old fogey like me.'

Nicholas Tempest's brows lifted. 'Then we shall have to find some means of keeping her entertained,' he said softly.

Cally freed herself hastily, murmured something about unpacking the groceries, and escaped. But even as she busied herself, stowing things away in the larder and the big old-fashioned refrigerator, she found herself assailed by the memory of the touch of his hand on hers. And scared by it too, in a way that was both unfamiliar and totally unwelcome.

And that, she thought tiredly, was how it had begun. Meeting him socially at dinners and parties in the locality, and when he came to visit her grandfather for reasons she'd never been able to fathom—not then. Occasionally she'd encountered him when she went riding, and he'd joined her astride a smart bay gelding that was a marked contrast to her own gentle, ageing Baz.

That had been the only time they'd ever met alone. Their conversation had always been general, and Cally had been astute enough to realise that she was being kept at a distance mentally as well as physically. Because he'd made no attempt to touch her again.

Yet before long she'd found herself looking out for him— hoping that she'd see him. Finding herself curiously at a loss when the business of his various companies had called him away. Shyly delighted when she'd learned of his return.

She'd never found the visits to Wylstone Hall much to her liking, particularly as Sir Ranald's widow Adele had still been snugly ensconced there, acting as Nick's hostess. Cally had been discomposed to find herself pinpointed by Lady Tempest's contemptuous violet gaze on more than one occasion, and the crimson lips had been quite capable of uttering limpid remarks, supposed to be teasing, yet designed to make Cally feel like a gauche schoolgirl. She'd found herself half-dreading those uncomfortable occasions.

'Says she doesn't want to be known as a dowager because it sounds so elderly,' Robert Naylor snorted after one of them. 'But Nicholas should pack her off to the Dower House just the same, and be quick about it—before the gossip starts. All this drooping around in black doesn't fool anyone, and I'd put money on her not having shed a single tear for poor Ranald. God only knows where he found her, but she's no intention of going back there.'

He shook his head. 'Wouldn't surprise me if she was banking on becoming Lady Tempest for a second time.'

'You mean Sir Nicholas might marry her?' Cally was startled in a number of ways, not all of which she wanted to examine too closely. 'But she's older than him.'

'Well, he's thirty, so there can't be more than a few years in it,' her grandfather said with a grunt. 'And she's a looker. I'll grant her that. No one could blame her for trying.' He gave another wag of the head. 'And proximity's a damned dangerous thing.'

'Yes,' Cally conceded with an odd feeling of numbness, 'I suppose it must be.'

Lying in bed that night, she thought of Adele, her beautiful face crowned by the sheen of her red-gold hair, her voluptuous body set off by the designer wardrobe that managed to make mourning seem a sexual experience. It was whispered locally, with nods and winks, that it was her excessive physical demands which had hurried her late husband into a relatively early grave.

'There's a woman who won't want to find herself in an empty bed,' was a remark Cally had overheard in the village shop.

But perhaps she isn't alone, Cally thought, lying awake, tormented by her imagination.

Looking back now, it seemed ludicrous that she could have been jealous of Adele.

But I was, she thought. And, being on my guard against her, I was diverted from seeing where the real danger lay.

Her unhappy musings were interrupted when she realised that Nick had once again turned off the motorway.

She sat up. 'Is this the right junction?'

'No, but it will do,' he returned briefly. 'I want to stop off in Clayminster first.'

He parked in a side street near the cathedral close and turned to her. 'Do you want to come with me?'

Cally examined a non-existent fleck on her nail. 'Thank you, no. I'd prefer to remain here.'

'Very well.' She watched him remove the keys from the ignition and pocket them. 'I won't be too long.' He paused. 'Please don't do anything stupid, or I might get angry.'

'God forbid,' she bit back at him. 'Why don't you have me electronically tagged?'

His mouth twisted in wry acknowledgement. 'I'll keep it in mind.'

Left alone, Cally examined and reluctantly discarded the idea of running away again. Both the bus and train stations, she knew, were right on the other side of town, and he would catch her before she'd gone half the distance.

Besides, in spite of her bravado, she didn't really want to make Nick angry, she admitted. The coming hours would be quite difficult enough without that. And sex as punishment was a terrifying possibility, which could destroy her, she thought, with a sudden convulsive shiver.

She got out of the car and stretched, then, leaving the door open, went for a restless stroll, up one side of the street and back down the other.

It didn't take long. It was mostly terraced housing, with a few shops, none of which tempted her to linger. A self-styled antiques gallery, offering mostly junk, was probably the star turn, she thought wryly, with a place called Needlewoman selling knitting wool and sewing requisites a close second.

Reaching the car, she leaned back against the doorframe with a sigh. The memories she'd allowed herself had been unsettling, reminding her of things best forgotten or treated as a temporary aberration.

I was just eighteen then, she thought blankly. A child trying not to fall in love with a man. And failing miserably.

In spite of the warmth of the day, she found she was wrapping protective arms round her body. Swallowing back the tears in her throat. Nick had said he would not be long, and she couldn't afford to let him find her crying.

It was another ten minutes before he turned the corner and walked up the street towards her, and by that time she'd managed to get a grip on her control and was sitting in the car again, waiting for him with a semblance of calm.

'I'm sorry,' he said as he joined her. 'It took longer than I expected.'

She didn't look at him. 'It's not important.'

'Ah,' Nick said quietly. 'But I think it is.' He took a jeweller's box from his pocket and opened it. She glanced at the contents and her eyes widened. She'd expected a ring, but the box contained a pair of them, in classic plain gold.

She said, 'Why two? In case I throw the first one away again?'

'No,' he said. 'The other one's for me.'

'For you?' She drew an uneven breath. 'That is—rank hypocrisy.'

Nick shook his head. 'It's a statement. Intended to make clear to any interested parties that our marriage is on again—and it's real.' He paused. 'Give me your hand.'

'I can put it on myself—if you insist that I must.'

'No,' he said. 'We'll do it my way.' He reached for her left hand, grasping it firmly. He said softly, 'I, Nicholas James Tempest, take you, Caroline Maria Maitland, for my wife.'

Half of her hoped that he'd got the sizing wrong, but the gold circlet slid easily over her knuckle.

He said, 'Now it's your turn.'

'This is ridiculous…'

'Cally.' His tone was gentle, but there was iron underneath. 'Say the words.'

Biting her lip, she obeyed, her low voice stumbling a little as she pushed the ring on to his finger in turn.

'Satisfied?' she challenged. 'I presume you don't want to add anything about for as long as we both shall live?'

His smile did not reach his eyes. He said quietly, 'Let's just say for as long as it's necessary, shall we?' He fitted the key into the ignition and started the engine. 'And now, my sweet wife, I'll take you home.'

CHAPTER FIVE

THE nearer they got to the village, the more Cally's inner tension increased. She found she was playing with the wedding ring, endlessly twisting it on her finger.

She'd done that before, she thought, a year ago as she'd paced the empty house, hearing the echo of her own footsteps, a ridiculous figure, the bride left alone on her wedding day.

And suddenly and terribly discovering why it should be so. Why Nick had chosen to leave her in solitude like that.

At the same time telling herself desperately that it couldn't be true. That Adele's words, still burning in her brain, had been sheer malice and spite. Nothing more.

That she couldn't—wouldn't take them seriously.

Yet knowing all the time that it was impossible to leave it there. Finding herself faced with the brutal necessity of discovering if her marriage was a deception—if the vows she'd exchanged with Nick only a few hours ago were utterly meaningless.

She made a small stifled noise in her throat, and was aware of Nick's swift glance.

'Are you all right?'

'Fine,' she lied. 'I was just thinking—wondering...' She paused, taking a deep breath. 'Whether we could make a quick detour to the cottage. Just for a few minutes.'

He was silent for a moment, then he said quietly, 'If that's really what you want.' And signalled for the turn on to the bottom road past the village.

He parked the car on the verge opposite the gate and Cally got out, trying not to look at the field beside them, which had once been Baz's paddock.

The shock of her grandfather's stroke, which had brought

her rushing back from her London job-hunt had been stressful enough. Baz's departure had been a very different kind of agony.

His stable at the rear of Oak Tree Cottage had already been demolished during her brief absence, and its timbers cut up for firewood. While the field where he'd grazed had been bought by a neighbouring farmer and ploughed for barley.

She'd been here, on this same spot, leaning on the fence, staring at the dark furrows and crying when Nick had found her.

'Cally.' His hands had been gentle on her shoulders, turning her to face him. 'What is it? Is your grandfather worse?'

'No. The doctors say he'll make a full recovery.' Her face was blurred and swollen with tears. 'But—he sold Baz while I was away. Got rid of him to some awful riding school in the North and never told me. He says that money's tight and we have to make savings.'

He was silent for a moment, then he said quietly, 'If you want to ride, you can use one of my horses.'

She shook her head. 'It's not that. You see, I've known Baz all my life—and he's just—gone. I can't believe it. I'm going to miss him so much.'

He'd said nothing more, she remembered. Simply drawn her close and held her. It was the first time he'd ever taken her into his arms, and she'd sobbed all down the front of his shirt. A child needing comfort rather than the woman she'd wanted to be.

She wondered suddenly if Nick remembered too, but knew she was being ridiculous. He was only interested in his own private vengeance. And besides, it all seemed such a long time ago.

She crossed the lane and unlatched one of the wrought-iron gates. It opened with a screech of rust. The path to the house was barely visible amid the weeds and coarse grass that flanked it.

And when she'd fought her way through the encroaching brambles there was little to see. Just the same sad pile of fire-blackened stones, from which she and her grandfather had escaped with nothing but their lives, she thought, shuddering.

She turned abruptly to go, and nearly cannoned into Nick, who had come quietly up the path behind her.

'Seen enough?' His hands descended on her shoulders, steadying her.

'It's still a ruin.' She freed herself, stepping backwards. 'I—I thought the whole place would have been cleared by now.'

'It's your ruin, Cally. The site belongs to you, and it's for you to say what should happen to it.' He paused. 'I thought you might want to rebuild. Provide yourself with a sanctuary for the future, when our marriage has finally ended.'

'No, thank you,' she returned coolly. 'I plan to be a long way off then.' She glanced back at the fallen walls and gaping windowframes. 'Too many bad memories here.'

'And not just for you,' he said abruptly, looking past her. 'Thank God I was driving past that night, and realised what was happening.'

'You took a terrible risk.' Her voice shook slightly. 'But I'd never have got my grandfather out without you.'

'What woke you?' he asked. 'Did you ever remember?'

She looked down at a broken flagstone. *I wasn't asleep. I was sitting on the window seat in my bedroom, thinking of you. Remembering how angry Grandfather had been when he saw you from his couch by the window, comforting me over Baz.*

'*Like father, like son.*' He sounded so bitter. '*Anything in a skirt. Keep out of his way, Cally, do you hear? He's no good for you. No good at all.*'

And I said, 'Yes, if that's what you want,' because I knew that anger was bad for him, and he needed to stay quiet and rest.

Aloud, she said flippantly, 'My guardian angel, I suppose. Who now seems to have deserted me.'

It had all seemed totally surreal, she thought, standing outside in the darkness as the fire service had fought the flames. As if she was looking at a medieval painting of an inferno. She still couldn't believe how quickly the fire had taken its hold. The heat had been intense, and the stench…

There'd been a sickening roar as the roof collapsed, and Nick had turned her in his arms, pressing her face against his shoulder so that she couldn't see how swift and overwhelming the destruction was.

'The ambulance is just leaving with your grandfather,' he'd whispered. 'There's nothing we can do here, so let me drive you to the hospital.'

And she'd nodded numbly, and allowed him to lead her away.

At the time she'd been too thankful to question what he'd been doing in the locality at that time of night. How he'd happened to be driving by. It was only much later that she'd realised Vanessa Layton's cottage also lay on the bottom road.

'A smoke detector might be more reliable than an angel another time.' Nick's dry tone forced Cally back into the painful present.

'I'm sure you're right.' She shook her head. 'I suppose I always knew the wiring was old and needed attention, but I didn't realise we were sitting on a time bomb.' She paused. 'Or that we had no insurance. It was quite a shock to find that we were homeless and penniless too.'

'Your grandfather was getting old.' Nick shrugged. 'It's easy to overlook these things.'

Not, she thought, when the company had sent constant reminders, and the cottage was desperately overmortgaged. But what was one more demand among so many? In spite of her distress about Baz, she'd seen why her grandfather had needed to sell him—and the land—to provide an urgent injection of cash, to stall their creditors. If Oak Tree Cottage hadn't burned down, they'd have only lost it in another way.

The horror of the fire had forced on her the discovery that they were broke. Not that her grandfather had ever been willing to discuss the situation, but she'd known she should have realised that all the signs were there, becoming more serious with every day that passed.

She said abruptly, 'I've seen enough, thanks. It—it was a mistake to come here.'

'Not altogether.' Nick opened the gate, allowing her to precede him. 'At some point you'll need to make a decision about the place.'

'At some point, yes.' She didn't look at him. 'Just now I have other things to worry about.'

It felt strange to drive through the village again. It seemed to her that she'd been away for a thousand years, yet nothing had changed. There weren't many people about, but she knew that the car had been spotted, and her presence noted. It wouldn't take long for word to get about that she'd returned.

Another nine-day wonder for the gossips to pick over, she thought wearily. And when she and Nick finally parted there'd be a feast for the wagging tongues.

Wylstone Hall stood in its own extensive grounds, and Cally could see instantly that a lot of work had been done there. Sir Ranald, in his latter years, had let the maintenance of the gardens slide, and Adele had taken no interest in it either.

But then she'd probably had other plans for what remained of her elderly husband's money, Cally thought with distaste.

Yet now the lawns had been cut and the trees pruned, while the formal flowerbeds had been replanted and were coming into bloom. Even the old fountain that stood in the middle of the broad gravelled sweep in front of the Hall's main entrance had been coaxed to work once more, and its showering droplets gleamed in the sunlight.

Wylstone Hall was a big, rambling place, more imposing than beautiful, combining a number of architectural styles from medieval to Victorian.

Cally had never found it particularly warm or welcoming, but was ready to concede this had probably been down to Adele and her hatchet-faced housekeeper.

The woman who now emerged to greet them as they got out of the car was a very different proposition, in her middle thirties, slim, and pleasant-faced.

'We're home, Margaret.' Nick drew Cally forward. 'Darling, this is Mrs Thurston, who'll help you all she can.'

'It will be a pleasure, sir, and welcome back. How do you do, your ladyship?' Her smile was anxious. 'There's something I should mention...'

'Later,' Nick said. 'And tell Frank to leave the bags for a while, too.' He looked down at Cally, said softly, 'I have an omission to repair. I broke with tradition the first time round, and failed to carry my bride over the threshold. Clearly a mistake.'

Before Cally could protest, or take any evasive action, he'd lifted her into his arms and started towards the entrance.

After the sunlight, the big hall felt cool and shadowy, and there was a scent of lavender in the air.

Cally realised that he was carrying her towards the sweep of the staircase. She said breathlessly, 'Nick—put me down.'

'In my own good time.' There was a note of amusement in his voice—and something else, infinitely more dangerous.

'Asserting your marital rights already, darling?' It was a woman's voice, low-pitched, drawling, and instantly unpleasantly familiar. 'And it's only just teatime. No wonder the poor child looks stunned.'

There was a frozen silence, then, slowly and carefully, Nick lowered Cally to the ground and turned.

'Adele,' he said expressionlessly. 'What an unexpected pleasure. I really thought you were in Paris.'

Adele Tempest remained where she was, framed in the doorway to the drawing room. She was wearing a close-fitting white skirt and a wrap-around top in a deep violet shade. Her redgold hair was piled on top of her head, with a few artless tendrils allowed to escape around her face and the nape of her neck. She was smiling.

'Oh, but I was,' she said. 'Then a little bird told me you were returning with the prodigal bride, and I thought at least one person should be here to welcome her. Apart from the servants, that is.' She looked Cally over, her smile widening. 'Nick's powers of persuasion must be overwhelming, my pet.

Or was it his money that you couldn't resist—yet again? After all, you've been living rough for a year now, and a fate worse than death probably seems marginally preferable to no fate at all.'

Cally kept her voice steady somehow. 'It's good to see you, too, Adele. And nice to know you haven't changed.'

Adele laughed. 'Oh, Nick's the one for alterations. You won't recognise the place since your last brief visit. I gather he's transformed that gothic horror of a master bedroom that Ranald was so stubborn about into a real love nest. Of course, I had no idea it was intended for you.'

'Well, life's just full of surprises,' Cally said lightly. She turned to the housekeeper, who was standing behind them, looking faintly agonised. 'Perhaps you'll show me this amazing transformation upstairs, Mrs Thurston? I'd like to tidy myself after the journey. And then we'll all have tea in the drawing room.' She smiled up into Nick's icy face. 'Please entertain our guest for me, darling. I won't be long.'

Without hurrying, she began to climb the stairs, following the housekeeper along the gallery at the top until they reached a pair of double doors, which Mrs Thurston threw open.

'This is the master suite, Lady Tempest. I do hope you'll be comfortable.'

Cally found herself in a large bedroom with pale walls and a low ceiling. There was a pretty Edwardian dressing table, with a satin stool, and apart from that the major piece of furniture was a four-poster bed, canopied in a rich dark blue edged with cream, with a matching quilted cover. The large windows were hung with the same fabric.

Cally forced a smile. 'It's—absolutely lovely.'

Mrs Thurston permitted herself a pleased smile, then hurried to open a door on the other side of the room, revealing a short passage, with more doors on either side.

'There's another bedroom at the end, which Sir Nicholas has been using up to now,' she announced. 'The dressing room, which is shared, is on the left, and the bathroom is directly opposite. If there's anything you need, you have only to ring.'

'I'm sure you haven't forgotten a thing,' Cally assured her.

The other woman hesitated. 'If I may say something, your ladyship? I—I'm really sorry about what happened downstairs just now. I knew Sir Nicholas wouldn't want any kind of intrusion today, but I didn't realise Lady Tempest was in the house.'

She shook her head. 'It was such a beautiful day, I opened the French windows in the drawing room. I suppose she walked across the garden from the Dower House and simply came up the terrace steps. I couldn't believe my eyes when I went in with the flowers and found her sitting on the sofa.'

Mrs Thurston paused. 'And, of course, she used to live here…'

'Which makes it doubly difficult to ask her to leave,' Cally supplied wryly. 'Please don't worry, Mrs Thurston. I'm sure my husband will deal with the situation.' She pulled a face. 'I suspect he's used to it.'

Mrs Thurston smiled dutifully, but she still seemed troubled as she left the room.

And why shouldn't she be? Cally asked herself, tossing her handbag on to the bed. I'm pretty troubled myself. Things are bad enough without Adele aiming her poison darts at every available target.

To find her waiting was turning the clock back with a vengeance.

She found her way to the bathroom, and washed her face and hands in cool water. It was the height of luxury, she thought, eyeing the creamy marble that tiled the walls and floor with reluctant appreciation. She was less certain about the big sunken bath and enormous shower cabinet, both of which looked as if they'd been deliberately designed for dual occupation.

What would she do if Nick insisted on those kind of intimacies? she wondered, her throat dry. What *could* she do?

When she emerged, she paused, then walked the few yards to the other bedroom and peeped round the door. With its double bed, in a fitted olive-green coverlet, and matching oak tallboys, it was a much plainer room, its ambience uncompromisingly masculine.

This was where Nick had been sleeping—when he slept at home. And maybe he would still choose to spend some of his nights here.

Her senses seemed to pick up the faint fragrance of the cologne he used, making his presence suddenly and formidably real, and she retreated hastily back to the master bedroom, feeling like Bluebeard's wife.

While she'd been in the bathroom their overnight bags had been brought up, and as she rummaged in her case for her brush and comb she saw the nightdress she'd worn the previous night was lying on top of the other things. She lifted it out, shaking the creases out of its folds, wondering whether or not she would be permitted to wear it tonight. Asking herself too, her stomach cramping nervously, exactly what Nick would expect from her.

In physical terms she knew what to anticipate, of course, although it was all theory without practice. And while she might resent the idea of his body invading hers, it wasn't particularly scaring. No, it was that extra emotional dimension that haunted her, made her curse her inexperience.

Not passion, she thought sombrely. That was too much for him to ask and he must know that. But certainly he would want…acquiescence, at the very least, and there was no certainty she could achieve that.

She sat down at the dressing table, drawing the brush through the silky tendrils of her hair before applying moisturiser to her skin and a touch of subtle colour to her mouth.

Warpaint, she thought with self-derision, wishing she had some chainmail to go with it.

She hesitated on the gallery leading to the stairs. All this part of the Hall was new to her. The room she'd occupied after the fire, while her grandfather had been kept in hospital, initially for observation, was at the other end of the house. She wasn't sure she'd ever be able to find it again in the twists and turns of the passages. Or that she even wanted to…

But she couldn't halt the relentless pressure of her memories.

On the night of the fire Adele's welcome, she recalled with a grimace, had been sugared, but her eyes had been unsmiling. And there had been no warmth either from the housekeeper who'd showed her upstairs.

It's not my fault, Cally had wanted to tell them both. She'd actually reached the hospital exit before she was stopped dead in her tracks by the realisation that her home didn't exist any more—or any of her belongings. That she had literally nowhere to go.

Nick's hand had closed on her arm. 'You're coming with me,' he'd stated, in a tone that brooked no argument, and almost meekly she'd allowed him to lead her to the car.

He must have telephoned ahead from Casualty, because the room had already been made up for her, and hot soup had been waiting on a table drawn up by the gas fire.

And Cally, to her own surprise, had found she was ravenous. She'd just put down her spoon when Adele had appeared.

'I've brought you a comb and a toothbrush,' she announced, handing over two cellophane-wrapped packets. 'And I suppose you'll need a nightgown.' She tossed something black and totally diaphanous on to the bed.

'Thank you,' Cally acknowledged woodenly, hiding her dismay. 'I'm sorry to put you to all this trouble.'

Adele shrugged. 'It's Nick's house now. He gives the orders. And being homeless must be ghastly.' She paused. 'If you leave your clothes outside the door, they'll be laundered ready for the morning. You can't wear them again like that. They absolutely reek of smoke.' She perched elegantly on the arm of the small fireside chair opposite. 'I suppose tomorrow you'll start looking for somewhere to rent, while all the financial stuff gets sorted?'

'Yes, I suppose I will,' said Cally, who couldn't look beyond the next five minutes. There'd be insurance, she thought. But could they afford to rebuild? Shouldn't they be trying to downsize instead? And could she ever persuade Grandfather to agree?

But she didn't want to think about that now. Her eyes were

stinging, her throat was dry, and her head felt as if it had been split with an axe. Unconsciously, she lifted a tired hand to rub her forehead.

'Headache, my pet?' Adele's tone sparked with malice. 'Well that's a tried and tested excuse. But I doubt it will cut much ice with your gallant rescuer.'

Cally looked at her wearily. 'I'm sorry, but I don't think I understand.'

'No?' Adele gave a light laugh. 'Well, I'm sure it will all be made clear to you pretty soon. In the meantime, I recommend a couple of aspirin. You'll find some in the bathroom cupboard.'

She rose and walked to the door with studied grace, leaving Cally to stare after her.

She shouldn't waste time worrying over the things Adele said or did, she told herself as she sought out the bathroom and the aspirin. The older woman was pure bitch, from her painted toenails to the top of her expensively coiffured head, and always would be. She was only sorry she was obliged to share a roof with her, even for one night.

The tablets swallowed, she ran herself a bath in the big old-fashioned tub, and sank with a sigh into clean hot water. She'd used nearly half a bar of lily-scented soap and a handful of shampoo before she began to feel human again.

She might not be too happy about being a guest at the Hall, but she was certainly going to be unhappy in luxury, she decided, looking at the deep pile of white fluffy towels awaiting her. She dried herself quickly, then wrapped a fresh bathsheet round her body, sarong-style, and covered her damp hair with a turban.

She trailed back into her room, and paused with a small gasp—because Nick was there, standing by the bed, examining Adele's nightdress with a sardonic expression.

'Your choice?' he enquired pleasantly, holding it up, making her acutely aware how sheer it was.

'Oh, no.' She was cross to find herself stammering slightly, and self-consciously readjusting her towel. 'I don't wear that kind of thing. I—I think Lady Tempest meant to be kind.'

'But not necessarily to you,' Nick said softly.

'What do you mean?' She was defensive.

'Don't be naïve, sweetheart,' he drawled. 'I imagine she thought you'd be wearing it for me.' And he watched the betraying wave of colour wash her face.

'But don't worry about it,' he added. 'I'll return it to her and try to find you something more appropriate. And tomorrow you can go shopping.'

He paused. 'However, what I really came to say is that the fire is now out, and the firemen have managed to salvage a big tin container from what's left of the dining room.'

'Oh—Grandfather's strong box!' She seized thankfully on the shift of focus. 'That—that's marvellous. It's got all his private papers in it, plus our passports, our birth certificates, the insurance documents. Everything. He'll be so relieved.'

He nodded. 'Now, try and get some sleep. It will all seem better in the morning.'

'Nick,' she said, as he reached the door. 'About tonight—I don't know how to thank you...'

'Now, I can think of all kinds of ways,' he said mockingly. He held up the nightdress. 'Perhaps I should ask you to model this for me, after all. Except that you have a lot on your mind right now, and I'd prefer your undivided attention.'

He watched her blush deepen angrily, and went off grinning.

Alone, Cally removed the turban and towelled her hair almost savagely. Adele might be vile, she thought, but Nick was no better. At one moment he could be so kind. Almost caring. The next he'd be hateful and teasing, putting her at a disadvantage and enjoying her embarrassment.

But perhaps it was safer that way, she told herself, biting her lip. Wasn't that why she'd tried to move to London—because she'd let herself hope that he cared about her in all the ways that mattered, and had come perilously near to making a total fool of herself?

She couldn't let that happen again.

Yet when a knock sounded at the door, some ten minutes later, she froze, wondering whether he'd stopped teasing and decided to return after all. And, if so, how she could best deal with it.

Dry-mouthed, she called, 'Come in…'

But it was only Mrs Bridges, looking boot-faced. 'I came for the dishes, miss,' she said. 'And Sir Nicholas sent you this.' She held out the man's white shirt that had been folded over her arm. 'He told me to say that it only came from Jermyn Street yesterday, so it's never been worn,' she added coldly.

'Oh.' Cally said. She took the shirt. 'Well—thank him for me, please.'

When the housekeeper had gone, she unwound the towel and undid enough buttons to enable her to pull the shirt over her head, shivering a little as she felt the crisp fabric graze the tips of her breasts and brush her naked thighs.

The sleeves were covering her hands, so she rolled them back a little, then turned and looked at herself in the mirror. She saw a girl with a pale face and dishevelled hair. Whose long bare legs under the formal lines of the shirt presented a strangely erotic image.

A girl whose shadowed eyes hid a secret she could not tell.

For a moment she allowed herself to wish that the shirt wasn't brand-new, but something Nick had worn. Something that might still bear the imprint of his body, or carry the scent of his skin in its fibres, so that for this one night she could pretend she was sleeping in his arms.

But that, she told herself, would be the greatest foolishness of all.

Sighing, she switched off the light and got into bed, and lay for a long time staring into a darkness that scared her by its loneliness.

'Lady Tempest?' Mrs Thurston's quiet voice brought Cally back to the present with a start. She spun round to see the other woman standing a few feet away. Clearly she'd been too lost in her painful memories to hear her approach. 'I'm sorry if I startled you, but I wanted to say that I've taken the tea into the drawing room.'

'Yes—yes, of course.' Cally mustered her thoughts and managed a smile. 'I was just trying to get my bearings—remember where I stayed when I first came here.'

Mrs Thurston looked puzzled. 'Excuse me, your ladyship, but I thought you lived in our flat.'

'That was later.' Cally led the way downstairs. 'When it became clear that my grandfather wasn't coming out of hospital.' She paused. 'I hope you find it as comfortable as I did.'

The other woman's face lit up. 'We couldn't be happier, your ladyship.' She paused awkwardly. 'But of course this has been a bachelor establishment up to now. You'll naturally be wanting to make changes.'

'Not for the foreseeable future,' Cally said, and smiled at her.

When she entered the drawing room, she discovered Adele was sitting alone, flicking through a magazine with undisguised boredom.

Cally checked in dismay. She didn't want to deal with the other woman alone. 'Where's Nick?'

'He decided not to be entertaining after all. He went off to take some phone call in his study and hasn't come back.' Adele's tone was short. 'He seems out of temper, Caroline dear. Perhaps he's finding this persistent virginity of yours a tad trying.'

Don't rise to the bait, Cally adjured herself, inspecting the tea table instead. There were tiny cucumber sandwiches, cut into triangles, plus a plate of scones, accompanied by dishes of jam and cream, and a tiered stand bearing a rich fruit cake, a Victoria sponge, and some shortbread.

Mrs Thurston seemed to be a treasure indeed, she thought gratefully.

She poured Adele's tea, with a slice of the requested lemon, and added milk to her own cup, then sat back taking an appraising look around her.

It was all entirely different. The heavy wallpaper had been

replaced by a creamy paint, and large comfortable sofas, their linen covers the colour of sand, had superseded the old-fashioned dark leather suite. Pale drapes hung at the long windows, and instead of the dreary carpet there were stripped and polished floorboards and Persian rugs. It was as if there'd been an explosion of light.

'Counting all the changes?' Adele asked, taking a sandwich. 'It'll take a long time.'

Cally shook her head almost wonderingly. 'The room seems to have doubled in size.'

'Well, at the Dower House I feel as if I'm living in a shoe-box,' Adele said shortly. 'And I've had to fight tooth and nail for the place to be made even habitable. In fact, that's one of the reasons I came up this afternoon—to ask Nick to send a carpenter round. Some of the upstairs window catches still don't fit properly.'

'I'll tell him about it.' Cally watched her. 'So, what was the other reason for your visit?'

Adele shrugged. 'Vulgar curiosity, my pet. I simply couldn't believe you'd swallowed your dubious pride and returned to Nick's eager arms after all. Proof, if proof were needed, that money always talks. You look a little careworn,' she continued. 'So I suppose the long-delayed consummation is scheduled for tonight.'

Her smile was cat-like. 'But I wouldn't worry too much. Your husband's an incredibly successful businessman, sweetie. I'm sure he's equally adept with women—especially nervous novices. You're the kind of challenge he'll enjoy—for a while. So I recommend you make the most of it,' she added with bite.

'Why, Adele—' Cally managed a laugh '—I do believe you wanted Nick yourself.'

But the older woman was unfazed. 'It would have been—convenient. God knows, Ranald left me hardly anything to live on. It was all tied up in trusts and entails. Too boring for words.' She shrugged again. 'But I simply wasn't prepared to ruin my figure providing Nicholas with the heir and the spare he clearly wanted. I'd already been through all that with Ranald. So he was forced to look around, and there you were.'

'Yes,' Cally said slowly. 'So I was.'

Adele gave a slight yawn. 'You can hardly blame him, after all the money he had to shell out to pay off your grandfather's creditors. He's no doubt made it plain to you where your duty lies. He wants a return on his investment, and pretty damned soon. I'd really make sure he gets it. Because he can be pretty ruthless when he tries.'

She drank the rest of the tea and put her cup on the table. 'And now I really mustn't intrude on this romantic idyll any longer.'

She rose and strolled towards the French windows. Then turned.

'By the way,' she added negligently, 'I understand Nick's— other interest has gone away for a week or two. Very diplomatic to absent herself while the reconciliation takes its course, don't you think? But don't hope for too much, because I warn you now—she'll be back. So you'll just have to learn to turn a blind eye, sweetie. Won't you? Because running away clearly hasn't worked.'

And with a last smile she was gone.

CHAPTER SIX

CALLY sat very still, staring in front of her. She was aware of a number of things—birdsong from the garden, the faint scent of the lilac that grew on the terrace, the clock ticking quietly on the mantelpiece—and yet at the same time she felt numb.

She looked down at her bare arms, almost surprised to find the skin unblemished. She'd half expected to see marks, scored into the flesh from Adele's talons.

Last time her own nails had etched crescents into the palms of her clenched hands as she'd stood listening, unable to speak or move away. She'd felt like some ancient city she'd heard of in history, which had been destroyed stone by stone and its earth sown with salt so that it would remain a barren waste.

But she'd been through that and survived—somehow. So why should she be remotely upset now at Adele's taunting remarks? After all, they were no surprise. She might have known Adele would not wait to put the boot in.

She shook her head. Could she possibly have been praying in some pathetic, hidden corner of her mind that Nick's affair might have ended during her absence? And that Vanessa Layton might even be gone—from the cottage, from the locality, from her life—never to trouble her again?

No, she thought, swallowing the lump in her throat. That had always been too much to hope for. And while Vanessa remained, she would always have priority with Nick, as Cally had learned in one bleak, agonising lesson on her wedding day. Even for twenty-four hours he'd been unable to pretend that his young bride took precedence over his mistress.

Vanessa had beckoned, and he'd gone running to her side, unable to keep away.

So now I'm the one who has to pretend, thought Cally, pain

lancing her. I'm the one who must learn not to ask who was on the phone, or where he's been, or what time he'll be home. Because they're all no-go areas.

A year ago I ran, because I couldn't bear it. Because I knew the only way to survive was to learn to live without him. But now I don't have that choice any more.

She tensed as the drawing room door opened.

'I can't believe it—you've managed to get rid of the Black Widow,' Nick commented, sounding faintly amused. He came slowly across the room and dropped on to the sofa opposite, lounging against the cushions. 'Did you murder her? If so, remember to put a stake through her heart before the burial.' He looked at Cally, his eyes narrowing. 'What the hell did she want, anyway?'

'A carpenter,' Cally said quietly. 'Something about window catches.'

His mouth twisted. 'Of course. With Adele there's always something.' He paused. 'Was that all?'

'What else should there be?' Cally enquired coolly. She indicated the table. 'Would you like some tea?'

'I did have other plans,' he said silkily. 'But they can wait.' He paused, waiting while she poured and then mutely handed him his tea. 'So, what do you think of the house?'

'Unrecognisable.' She looked around her. 'Also terrific. What prompted such a total makeover?'

'Because it was like living in a mausoleum,' he said. He gave her a level look. 'I also thought seriously about selling it, but I was persuaded this was the better option. I suppose time will tell.'

There was another silence, then, 'Did you like the bedroom?' he asked suddenly. 'I seem to recall you once told me that blue was your favourite colour.'

'Yes.' She bit her lip. 'I'm surprised you remember.' *Or even care...*

He shrugged. 'I've had damned little else to do,' he returned. 'And you've just given me strong tea with no sugar, so your memory's working equally well.' He smiled at her. 'You're clearly going to be the perfect wife.'

'But only,' she said clearly, 'for as long as it takes.'

His smile of acknowledgement was ironic. He reached for a sandwich. 'Was that really all Adele wanted?' he probed, after a pause. 'She pushed the knife in when we arrived, so I'm surprised she didn't decide to—twist it a little.'

Cally drank some tea. What could she tell him that he'd believe, without mentioning Vanessa?

She said quietly, 'She referred to Grandfather's debts. The implication was that you'd brought me back in order to exact your own brand of repayment.' She replaced her cup and saucer on the table. 'I could hardly deny it.' She lifted her chin. 'She's also worked out that I'm here to supply the next generation. I couldn't argue about that either.'

'I'm sorry,' Nick said abruptly.

'Why?' She shrugged. 'I should be used to her by now.'

'I'm sorry because I should have made sure she was out of the Hall well before our wedding.' His mouth twisted. 'But she wasn't easily dislodged. She even fought like a tigress to get me to appoint her as some kind of project manager. Boasted she'd have turned the place into a palace years ago if Ranald had given her the money. She'd even had plans drawn up for an indoor swimming pool at the rear, complete with a sauna and a Jacuzzi—and that was just for starters.

'Eventually I made it clear to her that I knew exactly the kind of background I wanted, and her creative input wouldn't be needed,' he added reflectively. 'Instead I turned her loose on the unfortunate Dower House.'

Cally took another look round, her brows lifting. 'You mean you did all this yourself?'

'I had help.' He hesitated. 'A—friend of mine used to be an interior designer.'

A friend of mine? A half-forgotten detail from Adele's story clawed suddenly at Cally's memory, telling her the friend's identity—as if she couldn't have guessed. *My bedroom,* she thought savagely. *Oh, God, that beautiful room. Did she—did*

Vanessa Layton suggest the décor for that? If so, it was cynicism carried to the ultimate degree—to prepare a place for her lover to sleep with his wife.

'The problem with Adele is that I can hardly evict her.' She became aware that Nick was speaking, his brows drawn together in a frown. 'As Ranald's widow, she's probably entitled to live at the Dower House for as long as she wants.' His frown deepened. 'I thought—I hoped—that once she stopped being lady of the manor she'd get bored out of her skull and move on. But no such luck.'

Cally pulled herself together, looking down at the golden gleam of her wedding ring. 'I gather she's strapped for cash.'

'She always was.' His mouth twisted. 'Maybe I should make her an offer she can't refuse.'

'Why not?' Cally went on staring at her ring, aware of its alien presence. 'It worked with me.'

His mouth twisted. 'With Adele, I lack quite the same leverage.' He'd finished his tea and was leaning back, long legs crossed. Completely at ease, it seemed. While she was in this unbelievable pain.

He said, 'I wondered, you see, after you'd gone, whether she could be part of the cause. If she'd said or done something to upset you. After all, there was no love lost between you. And I knew you were vulnerable—'

'Oh, spare me, please,' Cally broke in, her colour heightened hectically. 'Grandfather's death was hardly unexpected. The doctors warned us that the smoke inhalation—the stress of the fire—would probably lead to another stroke—and that it would be fatal.'

'Whether or not…' He paused. 'Cally, I know I shouldn't have left you alone like that, so soon after the wedding, but it was an emergency. Mrs Bridges was supposed to tell you that—to explain that I had to go out. I had no choice in the matter.'

Don't lie to me, she begged silently. It's too late for that. Because I know where you were. I went there. I heard you. Dear God, I saw you. With her.

'Cally.' Nick was leaning forward, his face serious. 'You're a million miles away. Please listen to me, because there's something I have to tell you. I—owe you an explanation.'

'No.' The word exploded out of her, and she saw the shock in his face, 'I mean—there's absolutely no need to say anything,' she went on, her tone hard and bright. 'Then or now. As they say—never apologise, never explain. And it's all fine—really. In fact, it was a blessing. As I said, it gave me a breathing space—a chance to reconsider what I'd done.' She gave a little laugh. 'Rather like being reprieved from a life sentence. So you did me a favour.'

His mouth hardened. 'Only now the shackles are once again in place. Is that what you're saying?'

'Your words,' she said. 'Not mine.'

'And you really don't want to hear what I have to say?'

'If I'd cared,' she said, with a shrug. 'I'd have been here when you got back.'

'Oh God,' he said with a kind of savage weariness. 'Cally, can we stop this and start behaving sanely.'

'This is hardly a rational situation.'

'Then let's make it one,' he said with sudden urgency. 'Let's wipe out the past twelve months as if they never existed. We're here—together—and we're married. Can't that be all that matters?' He paused. 'Besides, I have a wedding present for you.'

'A wedding present?' she echoed derisively. 'At the risk of sounding ungracious, I think I'll pass.'

He was very still. 'The bridegroom's gift to the bride,' he said slowly. 'It's a tradition.'

She lifted her chin defiantly. 'You're big on those, suddenly. But it makes no difference. Your generosity tends to come with too high a price tag, Sir Nicholas.'

He was silent for a long moment, his eyes narrowed. He said quietly, 'You don't even want to know what it is—my gift? You've no wish to see it?'

'None.' She took a swift breath. 'Can't you see I want nothing from you? Don't you understand that the only thing of value you could give me is my freedom—and the absolute certainty that I'll never have to see you again? But I doubt that's on offer.'

'Not immediately.' His voice was harsh. 'However, I can probably arrange matters so that we only meet in bed. Perhaps that might make your sentence easier to bear. Although we will have to share occasional meals,' he went on. 'Starting with dinner tonight, which I've arranged for eight-thirty. And you, my sweet wife, will sit at my dining table and pretend to enjoy the special food that Margaret is preparing. And, to enter fully into the spirit of the occasion, you will wear your wedding dress, which you'll find with the rest of your things upstairs in the dressing room.

'And that's not a request,' he added swiftly, as her lips parted in protest. 'It's an order.'

There was a corrosive note in his voice that frightened Cally.

This was a dynamite situation, she realised, and she hadn't handled it well.

'And now I'll respect your wishes and leave you in peace, to enjoy your own company.' He got to his feet. 'As usual, there's some work I should do. After all, I need to work harder, don't I, darling? Earn more money now that I have a wife to support and the prospect of a child.'

'Nick,' she said, her voice shaking. 'Nick—please.'

At the door, he turned. 'Having regrets, sweetheart?' His tone was ice. 'Save them for bedtime. You might just need them.'

Alone, Cally sat for an endless moment, staring at the closed door. She could still feel his anger in the room—an almost tangible bitterness, making the walls close in on her. Making it suddenly difficult to breathe.

She rose and ran across the room, half stumbling in her haste, to the French windows and out on to the terrace, where she paused, gasping.

How dared he treat her like this—speak to her in that way? she demanded silently as she leaned against the stone balustrade, trying desperately to compose herself. She'd run from him on an impulse triggered by shock and grief, because her life had suddenly become unbearable, but he was the cause of that. It was his fault, not hers. She'd been forced to go. She'd had no other choice.

And even if she'd stayed—forced a confrontation—it would have led to the same result in the end.

Had he really believed he could keep his mistress a secret from her? she wondered. True, Southwood Cottage was in a sufficiently isolated spot to provide a discreet rendezvous. But even if Adele hadn't told her about the affair there'd have been gossip—hints—eventually. In a small locality that was inevitable. And the longer their marriage had existed, the worse the sense of betrayal would have become.

During lovemaking did he say the same things—do the same things as he did with her? Those were things she would have asked herself over and over again, torturing herself in the knowledge that she would never find an answer that gave either comfort or hope.

And did he draw comparisons between them?

Perhaps he'd thought she'd be so besotted with him by that time—so dazzled and indulged with sex and money—that she'd be unwilling or unable to give him up. That she'd be prepared somehow to share him.

She might also—heaven help her—have been carrying his child, which would have reduced her options still further.

But this was no longer a hypothetical situation, she thought, shivering. It was going to happen, and she would have to find some way to live with it. To endure…

Her fingers tightened convulsively on the stone ledge. 'Don't go there,' she whispered to herself.

At least this time around limits had been imposed on her unhappiness. And, as long as she could keep its root cause hidden, she had a chance of emerging from the whole disaster with her pride battered but intact, if nothing else.

There is something I have to tell you.

Not while I have breath, Cally thought fiercely. Confession may be good for the soul, but not when my heart has to be torn apart as a consequence. I don't need this belated honesty.

Get FREE BOOKS and a
FREE GIFT when you play the...

LAS VEGAS
GAME

*Just scratch off
the gold box with a coin.
Then check below to see
the gifts you get!*

YES! I have scratched off the gold box. Please send
me my **2 FREE BOOKS** and **gift for which I qualify.** I understand
that I am under no obligation to purchase any books as
explained on the back of this card.

306 HDL D7YX   **106 HDL D7ZY**

FIRST NAME   LAST NAME

ADDRESS

APT.#   CITY

STATE/PROV.   ZIP/POSTAL CODE   (H-P-12/05)

7	7	7	Worth TWO FREE BOOKS plus a BONUS Mystery Gift!
🍒	🍒	🍒	Worth TWO FREE BOOKS!
🔔	🔔	♣	TRY AGAIN!

www.eHarlequin.com

Offer limited to one per household and not
valid to current Harlequin Presents®
subscribers. All orders subject to approval.

The bride's present to the groom—forgiveness and absolution. Was that really what Nick was hoping for?

Or had he simply realised the impossibility of maintaining the secrecy of his liaison for much longer? And was he crazy—or just cruel—to think that bringing the issue into the open would somehow make it easier to deal with? If so, how wrong could anyone be?

'Her name's Vanessa Layton.' The image of Adele's slow smile came back to haunt her as her mind went into freefall. The confrontation had taken place in the hall, and for some strange reason Cally could remember a bowl of early roses standing on a side table, and the soft whisper as one of them shed its petals. There'd been a shaft of sunlight coming through the open front door, hitting her as if she was a small animal caught in the headlights of a car. Rendering her transfixed—immobile.

'She was an interior decorator in London, and a good one, by all accounts. Nick hired her to redo his flat, and that's when it began. It must have been a pretty torrid affair for her to abandon everything, and let him install her in a dead and alive hole like Southwood Cottage,' she went on, her eyes carelessly surveying the pale, stupefied face of the girl in front of her. 'Clearly they can't bear to be apart. And she doesn't pay rent like an ordinary tenant, besides which Nick picks up all her bills.'

From some unsuspected well of courage Cally recovered the power of speech. 'How do you know this?'

Adele shrugged. 'The paperwork's all there in his desk, if you don't believe me. I happened to see it months ago, when I was looking for something else.'

'You were snooping.'

'Was I? Anyway, it's in the top right-hand drawer. Unless, now he's married, he's decided to move the evidence to somewhere less accessible. After all, he won't want to upset the apple cart.'

Cally said hoarsely, 'If it's all so wonderful, why hasn't he married her?'

'Because there's already a husband, apparently, but no one knows quite where. Maybe divorce isn't an option, for some reason.' Adele shrugged again. 'But for many reasons Nick needs a wife.' Her smile widened. 'And that, my pet, is where you come in, of course. Young, free, and clearly besotted. Central casting couldn't do better.'

There was a silence, then Cally said quietly, 'You utter bitch.'

Adele looked amused. 'I'm trying to be your friend here. After all, she'll only be the first of many, so you'd better be prepared. Nick's father was just the same,' she added insouciantly. 'No woman was safe around him. He left a string of broken hearts and marriages wherever he went, including his own. Why do you think your mother-in-law resumed her career so suddenly? Because she was sick of the endless betrayals, and scandals, and everyone knew it.'

Her smile widened. 'Jungles with wild animals and poisonous snakes must have seemed a soft option compared with Nick Tempest senior.'

Like father, like son. Her grandfather had said that. Had he known—heard gossip that Nick was involved with a married woman? Was that why he'd tried to warn her off?

'Besides,' Adele continued, 'I feel so sorry for you, moping round the house, waiting for Nick to come back and relieve you of your virginity. Especially when he's off consoling his bit on the side. Reassuring her that it's just a marriage of convenience, and it's business as usual as far as she's concerned.'

'And you're also unforgivably vulgar,' said Cally, and went past her, through that open door and out of the house. She was shaking so much she thought she might fall in pieces, but she made herself keep moving.

Somehow she made her way to the flat in the courtyard which, until that day, had been her home. The rooms were already empty, as blank as if they'd never been occupied. The bed in her room had been stripped, and only a few clothes remained in the cupboards and drawers. But her bag was still there, with her wallet and her bank book. She'd been intending to come and collect it, but then she'd been intercepted by Adele. She glanced inside, checking the car keys were there, too. That she had what she needed. Except she had no real idea of where she was going, or what she would do when she arrived.

She thought, Whatever happens, I have to know. Have to...

She unbuttoned the ivory silk dress she was still wearing from the morning's ceremony and stepped out of it, discarding the pretty lacy undies beneath as well. She found a cotton bra and briefs, that she'd considered far too workaday for her new life, and covered them with a denim skirt and a white T-shirt, sliding her feet into a pair of elderly sandals.

The bride was gone, and only a girl with a white face and burning eyes was left.

She'd only had the car for a week—a sleek, sporty Alfa Romeo that had been Nick's gift to her. She knew where Southwood Cottage was, of course. She could remember once catching a fleeting glimpse of its occupant, too. A dark-haired woman, she recalled, with one of those serene Madonna-like faces, working in the garden. Proving that appearances could be deceptive.

A saint in the kitchen, but a whore in the bedroom, she thought as she slid into the driving seat. Wasn't that supposed to be every man's idea of the perfect woman? She found she wanted to laugh hysterically, and sat for a moment regaining her self-control before starting the car.

When she reached the lane where the cottage was situated, she parked at its top and walked the rest of the way.

As she'd driven, she'd prayed that it wasn't true. That Adele was playing some kind of obscene joke on her. But Nick's car was there, under the shelter of some trees. There could be no mistake.

Cally moved quietly along the verge. As she reached the corner of the white-painted fence she heard voices. Hating herself, trembling violently, she crouched, looking through the branches of a tall shrub, and saw her worst fears confirmed. Nick was there, in the garden, standing with Vanessa Layton in his arms. She was clinging to him and crying, and he was stroking her hair.

'It's going to be all right.' He spoke quietly, but his voice carried easily to where Cally was hiding. 'Darling, I'll always be there for you.'

Cally couldn't hear her reply, but she watched Nick glance swiftly at his watch and nod. Together, they walked to the front door and went inside, closing it behind them.

Cally got shakily to her feet, then froze as Nick appeared at what was obviously an upstairs bedroom window.

Don't let him see me, she begged silently. She shrank into the shelter of a tall tree which was throwing a grotesque shadow on the road. Don't let him find me spying on him. Haven't I been humiliated enough without that?

Then she saw his hand move, realised he was drawing the curtains. Closing them in together. And that her concern was wasted, because he was clearly oblivious to everything but the woman going back into his arms in the shadowy room.

Suddenly she was aching inside, as if she'd been knocked down and kicked. Only bruises would heal eventually. Her wound was deep enough to be mortal, and she had to get away before she bled to death.

Uncaring whether she was seen or not, she stumbled back to her car. Her throat was dry and her eyes were burning, but she couldn't cry. That would come later, at a point she couldn't even envisage yet.

She only knew that her life was sick, cold and empty, and that there was nothing left for her here. That her betrayal was as cruel as it was complete.

I can't face him, she thought. I can't let him see what he's done to me. I can never do that. It would destroy me.

Young, Adele had said, and besotted. She'd failed to mention abysmally, unforgivably stupid, although the implication had probably been there.

And now, somehow, she had to save herself from further folly. And that meant distancing herself from Nick, as far and as fast as she could. Hiding out somewhere until enough time had passed for her to demand that the marriage be legally and immediately terminated.

And I did it, Cally thought now, lifting her face to the sun. I ran away. First to London, to cover my tracks and empty my account of any money there was. Thereafter by dint of sticking a pin in a map.

She'd been so sure he'd want to be rid of her as quickly and quietly as possible, without further damage to his male pride, and he'd agree to anything she asked when they finally caught up with each other.

Yet how wrong could anyone be? Because here she was, back at Wylstone—and on his terms, not hers.

Living with him, sharing his bed, and ultimately giving him a child. Those were the requirements she had to fulfil. And she would need every scrap of icy indifference that she could conjure up merely to survive.

Because, in spite of everything Nick had done, and all the reasons he'd given her to hate him, Cally was not sure, even now, that she could wholly trust herself where he was concerned.

In fact, she realised that she could be on the verge of a totally catastrophic self-betrayal.

From the moment they'd met she'd been aware of a dark, bewildered excitement stirring deep within her. Every time he'd looked at her, or smiled or spoken, it had seemed as if a silken thread was drawing her ever deeper into a maze of confused emotion she was too inexperienced to understand.

And the terrible damning truth was that nothing had changed.

It had been that day by the river when she'd first acknowledged his potential power over her. It had not, however, been the first time she was aware of it, but her consciousness had been submerged by all the sudden, overwhelming changes which had overtaken her.

The shock of her grandfather's death had been enough to cope with. And then she'd found herself knocked sideways with the news of the financial morass he'd left behind. She'd still been stunned and grieving when Nick had asked her to marry him—except that his quiet, contained words had been less a proposal than a statement of intent, which had told her there was no need to be frightened of the future, because he would look after her.

She'd found herself longing with utter thankfulness to throw herself into his arms and feel them holding her in safety against the world. Just when everything seemed lost, all the dreams she'd ever had were coming true. She hadn't been able to see further than that.

She'd allowed him to take charge, making no demur when he suggested that in view of her recent bereavement they should have a completely private early-morning wedding, with the vicar's wife and the verger as their only witnesses.

No Adele, she'd thought, her heart lifting. Just the two of us.

But, however quiet the ceremony, she'd still been determined to wear a special dress, and she'd found one in a Clayminster boutique, designed simply in plain ivory silk, short-sleeved, with a soft swirling skirt and a V-necked bodice fastened by a row of tiny-silk covered buttons.

And Nick, in turn, had insisted on a traditional honeymoon, even if it meant working long hours to clear his desk in preparation.

In the fortnight leading up to the wedding she'd hardly seen him at all, so it had been a major surprise when he'd arrived at the flat one sunlit afternoon, only a couple of days before the ceremony, and announced he was taking her on a picnic.

It had occurred to her, as she changed into shorts and a white cotton shirt, that this was the first time since he'd proposed to her that they would be alone together for any length of time, and she'd felt her throat close in excitement and trepidation.

He'd found them a sheltered spot under a tree, a few yards from the water's edge, and spread out a rug and cushions. The food had been simple enough—cold chicken, crusty bread, cheese, fruit and a bottle of wine—but Cally had thought she'd never tasted anything so wonderful.

Nick, stretched out beside her, had been relaxed and un-alarming, his grey eyes warm with laughter as he chatted to her about everything and nothing, making her forget her shyness as she responded to him.

'I think we should drink a toast,' he said at last. He filled her glass with wine and handed it to her. 'To us. Soon to be man and wife.'

She tried to raise her glass with similar smiling insouciance, but suddenly the significance of what marriage to him was going to mean came home to her, and her hand jerked nervously, disastrously, sending most of the wine down the front of her shirt.

'Oh God, I'm so clumsy.' She grabbed at a napkin, but his hand took her wrist and held it. She saw his grey gaze turn smoky, and, glancing down, saw what he was seeing. The damp shirt was clinging to the delicate uplift of one rounded untrammelled breast, outlining the nipple—revealing her as if she were naked.

'Cally.' His whisper of her name was husky. He moved, taking the dripping glass from her hand, pulling her into his arms. His mouth brushed hers lightly and sweetly, the tip of his tongue exploring the curve of her lower lip, probing gently, while the long fingers encompassed her breast with a sensuous purpose that sparked an answering tremulous ache deep within her.

Helplessly, she felt her nipple rise and harden under the stroke of his thumb, and her head fell back against his supporting arm, allowing his lips to travel down the line of her throat to the opening of her shirt. Tantalisingly, he allowed them to hover there for a long moment, the warmth of his tongue caressing the cleft between her breasts as if he was sipping the spilled wine from her skin.

Then he moved back, to put his mouth to hers, parting her lips with pleasurable mastery. His kiss was deep and unasham-edly sensual, and her body arched against his in involuntary response, her breast thrusting avidly against the subtle play of his fingers.

Still kissing her, he slid his hand down to her bent leg, caressing her bare knee then sliding upwards with aching slowness over her thigh to the edge of her brief shorts, where he paused. She felt the breath catch in her throat as the moment became endless—unendurable. As her ungiven body clenched suddenly in a need she'd never experienced before.

'Darling.' He raised his head to look down at her. There was a note in his voice she'd never heard before either. A look in his eyes she'd never seen, making her weak—molten with longing. 'My beautiful girl...'

He bent to kiss her again, then tensed, turning his head sharply and listening. And Cally heard it too—in the distance, but fast approaching—the high-pitched barking of a dog.

Nick sat up, pushing the dishevelled hair back from his forehead, then lifting Cally so that her back was against the trunk of the tree. He handed her back her glass. 'We seem to have a visitor,' he said, his voice laconic.

The dog, a Jack Russell terrier, came bundling across the grass towards them, his stump of a tail wagging furiously. He paused a few feet away, still yapping excitedly, then sat up, waving his paws in the air.

Cally could hear voices calling, and someone whistled, but the dog stayed where he was, bright eyes fixed on the remains of the picnic.

'So you have to be paid to go away, is that it?' Nick sounded amused. He tore off a piece of chicken and tossed it to the dog, who wolfed it down eagerly. 'Now clear off,' he added. 'If you know what's good for you, you appalling mutt.'

The dog gave the food another long, regretful look, before deciding to reluctantly obey the increasingly agitated whistling and trotting off.

Silence returned, but it had changed to a different kind of quietude. The bark of the tree felt rough through Cally's thin shirt as she leaned against it, eyes closed, attempting to control her breathing. And to hide, she realised, her sick disappointment. Because the moment had passed, and she knew it with a pang of utter desolation.

As if in unspoken confirmation, Nick's hand touched her cheek lightly, fleetingly. He said gently, 'I think it's time I took you home.'

'Yes.' She forced a smile, brightness into her voice. 'It—it's getting late.' She knelt, helping to pack the hamper, avoiding looking at him directly.

When they reached the Hall, Nick accompanied her across the courtyard to the door of her flat, and she felt herself tense as she lifted the latch, wondering whether he would ask to come in. And, if so, whether he would stay...

But she was soon disabused of that notion.

'I'll say *au revoir*,' he told her almost abruptly. 'I'm driving up to London this evening. I have a few loose ends to tie up.' He took her hand, brushing its knuckles in a swift kiss, even the gesture seeming to distance him. 'So—see you in church.'

She smiled, and nodded, and went inside, closing the door. Deep within her she was still shaking, her body an ache of yearning. She leaned back against the heavy panels of the door and closed her eyes.

'Two days,' she whispered, touching her fingertips to the sensitised fullness of her lower lip. 'Only two days...'

Oh, God, Cally thought now, with sudden violence. How many more times must I remember? Nick—my almost lover.

And how cruel that those few hours were her most vivid memory, every detail as sharp-cut in her mind as if it had happened minutes rather than months before.

But perhaps in this instance she needed total recall, she thought. Needed to remind herself how quickly she'd fallen under his spell, and how easily he could have seduced her.

Something Nick might well have thought of, too. And this time he'd make sure they weren't interrupted.

Shivering, Cally moved away from the balustrade and descended the steps to the lawn.

She'd asked herself a thousand times why he'd even bothered. He'd already been involved with a beautiful, experienced woman, so her innocence could hardly have constituted a turn-on for him.

But perhaps he'd planned the whole incident to test her capacity for arousal, she thought. To discover how much pleasure he could expect from his enforced nights with his brand-new wife.

That afternoon by the river, she would have given herself to him with total completeness, holding nothing back. And he knew that, she told herself, biting her lip.

I should have taken you while I had the chance. His own cynical words. And he would soon find out how right he'd been.

Because now she had to make some plans of her own. To make him understand in the bleakest terms that she wasn't the same person any more, and he was no longer her hero, riding to her rescue.

She had to reject the kisses and caresses that belonged to someone else and fight him, tooth and nail, to maintain her integrity.

All he would possess was the shell of the girl she'd once been. Nothing more.

And somehow, somewhere, she would hide all traces of the long, lonely hunger for him that still burned within her.

However he used her, that was something that Nick Tempest could never be allowed to know. And she shivered at the prospect of all the long nights ahead of her.

CHAPTER SEVEN

IN SPITE of her inner turmoil, Cally was unable to ignore the beauty of her surroundings for long. She had to admit that the grounds were looking at their best, poised on the verge of summer, and the scent of the grass and newly turned earth brought a kind of peace.

But only for a while. As she wandered restlessly across the lawns, the sun warm on her back, she found herself imagining that the past months had rolled away as if they'd never existed, and Nick was walking beside her, his fingers laced with hers, talking softly, his mouth and eyes smiling as sometimes he paused to kiss her. The way she'd once dreamed it might be.

Crazy, she thought, giving herself a mental shake. I'm going completely crazy. Living in never-never land.

As she reached the formal garden she saw that an elderly man was working with a hoe on one of the borders, and he straightened, beaming, as she approached. 'Good to see you, Miss Caroline. Beg pardon—Lady Tempest, I should say,' he added hastily.

Cally smiled back. 'Miss Caroline is just fine, Mr Robins. I can't get used to anything else. But I didn't know you were working at Wylstone.'

He looked faintly embarrassed. 'Six months or more now, your ladyship, and I've two lads to train as well. Things move on, you know, and a lot of the people I used to work for, like your grandpa, aren't here any more, so I'm glad of the security.' He nodded. 'He's a good man to work for, Sir Nicholas.' He paused. 'On your way to the stables, I dare say?'

'Oh—er—yes,' said Cally, her mind on other things. *A good man to work for...* Was that a way of surviving the months to

come? she wondered wryly. To regard herself somehow as just
another employee of a generous boss?

Maybe it was—if she could only keep her wayward and
futile dreams safely under control, she thought, suppressing an
unhappy sigh.

She said goodbye, and found herself turning towards the stables. She'd not planned a visit there, but it was either that or
return to the house. And she wasn't ready for that. Or not yet.

There was no one about in the yard, and she followed the
worn track down to the paddock, shading her eyes against the
sun, which was sinking towards the treetops now.

There were three horses turned out in the field. Two were
grazing quietly together, and the third stood alone in the far
corner, head down, tail swishing wearily against marauding
flies.

Cally, resting her arms on the fence rail, stared across at the
solitary horse. There was something about him, she thought
with bewilderment—his stance, maybe, or his colour—that was
strangely familiar.

As if aware of her scrutiny, he lifted his head and began to
move towards her across the paddock, his speed increasing as
he approached, whickering softly. And, she'd swear, joyfully.

Which was when she knew for certain. And the world
blurred.

'Baz,' she whispered chokingly. 'Baz, my beauty—my wonderful old boy.'

As she climbed the fence to get to him, her dress caught on
a splinter and she wrenched it free, uncaring. She stood beside
him, her wet face buried in his neck, one hand stroking his
muzzle as he lovingly nosed her shoulder and arm, waiting for
the expected treats as if it was only yesterday that they'd
parted.

'I've nothing with me.' She was laughing through her tears.
'No carrot, no apple. Because I—didn't know.'

I have a wedding present for you...

The one gift that Nick knew she could not refuse. Dear God,
but he was clever, she thought shakily.

She climbed on to the middle rung of the fence and swung herself on to Baz's back, holding his mane as she encouraged him to amble gently round the perimeter of the paddock.

The circuit was almost completed when Cally saw a girl standing at the gate, watching anxiously.

'Lady Tempest?' she asked as Cally brought Baz to a halt and slid to the ground. 'I'm Lorna Barton, the groom. I'm so sorry. I should have been here, but I thought you weren't coming after all, so I went up to the house for a cup of tea.'

'Well, it wasn't planned. As you see, I'm hardly dressed for riding.' Cally indicated her torn dress with a faint grimace. 'It was more of a happy reunion.'

Lorna's face relaxed. 'He's a grand old lad, isn't he? But never exciting enough for that riding school.' She shook her head. 'A couple of lessons and they all thought they were three-day eventers and wanted rides to match. So poor old Baz was surplus to requirements. I don't know what would have happened if Sir Nicholas hadn't found him, because no one was bothering with him.'

Cally hesitated. 'When was that, exactly?'

'About a year ago, and Sir Nicholas hired me to come with him.' Her rosy face acquired a deeper hue. 'He bought Baz for you, Lady Tempest, or so I understood. Only...'

'Only I wasn't here,' Cally supplied calmly. 'However, I'm back now, and I'll be exercising him regularly.' She paused. 'I presume he's up to it?' she added cautiously. 'He looks so much older.'

'He had a bad time in Yorkshire,' the other girl said sadly. 'And the vet's not totally happy about him even now. But he likes to be ridden, as long as it's not too far or too fast.'

'I'll be careful,' Cally nodded. 'And I'll see you tomorrow.' She ran a caressing hand down Baz's neck. 'Both of you.'

And now, she thought as she walked away, the breath catching in her throat, she would have to find Nick and thank him. She could do nothing else.

His study was at the back of the house. Cally knocked at the door, and waited until she was told to enter.

Nick was sitting behind a large oak desk, operating a laptop with frowning concentration. His tie was gone, and his white shirt was open at the neck, the sleeves turned back over his tanned forearms. He did not look up and his voice held a touch of impatience. 'Yes?'

She said, 'I just took delivery of my wedding present.'

His head lifted sharply. His grey gaze scanned her, taking in the flushed cheeks, the brilliance of excitement in her eyes, lingering over the ripped skirt.

He said, after a pause, 'You said you weren't interested.'

She shook her head. 'I just never dreamed...' Her voice thickened, and she swallowed. 'It's so wonderful to see Baz again, and Lorna says you pretty much saved his life. How—how did you find him?'

'You asked me to go through your grandfather's papers after his death. I found the bill of sale amongst them.'

'And you didn't say a word?'

He shrugged. 'No, but I remembered how upset you were, and I wanted to surprise you—make you happy.' He gave her a level look. 'But, as you know, I was the one destined for the surprise.'

She thought of the way he'd held her that day beside the empty field—comforted her—and, in spite of herself—felt her skin warm.

She bit her lip. 'Yes—well. I—I don't know how to thank you.'

Nick pushed back his chair and stood up, walking round the desk.

His voice slowed to a drawl. 'Now, I can think of any number of ways.' He leaned back casually against the edge of the desk and held out a hand. 'Come here.'

She supposed she should have expected it, but, stupidly, she hadn't.

Sudden nervousness knotted in the pit of her stomach. She said too quickly, 'You're busy. I—I shouldn't have interrupted.'

'There's nothing that can't wait.' He waited too, then sighed. 'Cally, don't make me fetch you.'

Reluctantly, she crossed the room and stood in front of him, looking down at the carpet. Nick reached out and took the hand she didn't offer, and then the other, drawing her towards him between his legs until their bodies touched.

She stood, silent and motionless, helplessly trapped by the long hard length of his thighs. Aware of the warmth of him through her thin dress. Still unable to meet his gaze.

Behind her ribcage she could feel the frantic flutter of her heart like a caged bird throwing itself against its bars.

He said softly, 'Darling, look at me.'

Her lashes felt weighted over her unhappy eyes, but she made herself obey.

'Nick—please,' she whispered. 'Not here—not like this…'

His voice roughened. 'What the hell do you think I want?'

'I—I don't know.'

'You talk about gratitude,' he said slowly, 'but you don't show it. Is one kiss really so much to ask—from a wife to her husband?'

He released her hands, touching her shoulders instead. Letting his fingers slide down her back to her hips and rest there.

'At our wedding you kissed me,' he told her quietly. 'All these months I've remembered the sweetness of your mouth. Kiss me again, Cally, just as you did that morning. And don't pretend you've forgotten.'

Forget? She wanted to cry aloud, as agony wrenched her. How could she possibly forget, when every detail of that day had been tormenting her—scarring her mind—ever since? Especially that moment when their lips had met to seal their vows.

Her innocence, she thought, offered freely and gladly to his passion. A girl anticipating with eagerness and trust the moment when the glorious alchemy of sex would transform her into a woman.

But only for a few brief hours—and then the dream had died.

She said coolly, 'We all remember things in different ways. Perhaps to me it was no big deal, and that's when I realised that gratitude was never going to be enough and decided to get out.'

He said harshly, 'Then I'll just have to take what little there is.'

His mouth was hard and sudden on hers, imposing a bleak sensuality that found her totally unprepared. She tried to struggle, but there was no evading the ruthless mastery with which he parted her lips, his tongue flickering like a flame against hers.

He turned her slightly, so that she was supported by his arm while one hand closed on the swell of her breast, his fingers stroking her nipple with almost casual expertise and, in spite of the barriers of cloth and her instant shocked recoil, bringing it to aching, irresistible life.

She tried to say no, but the word was stifled in her throat—lost against the pressure of his lips.

His kiss deepened relentlessly, exploring the inner contours of her mouth with the intensity of a connoisseur. Drained and dizzy, she could hardly breathe. She couldn't think any more, or muster any kind of emotional defence against the plundering lips, or the long, slow sweep of his hand down every curve and plane of her body.

And realised in some drowning corner of her mind that he would know that all too well.

That the battle was over, and he'd won...

At last he raised his head and looked down at her as she lay slumped and panting against him. The grey eyes were almost silver, heavy with desire, as, without haste, his fingers penetrated the jagged rip in her skirt, tearing it even further. As they caressed the silken flesh of her thigh, then softly teased their way along the lace edge of her underwear.

The breath caught painfully in her throat as Cally, tantalised to the edge of endurance, felt the sudden unequivocal surge of her body's response. The searing, incalculable need she had believed she'd overcome.

Deep inside her, a fist seemed to clench painfully, releasing the first scalding rush of passion. Demanding that the hunger he'd awoken should be appeased. And soon.

Imploringly, her lips tried to shape his name, and her hand went up to grip the front of his shirt, to draw him down to her again—to her waiting, trembling mouth. And then—and then to the molten eager heat of her first surrender.

But instead, his slow, intimate incitement was deliberately stilled, then withdrawn. And Cally found herself being lifted back on her feet and carefully steadied as Nick looked down at her flushed, strained face and shook his head slowly.

'Much as it grieves me, my sweet, I have to let you go.'

He didn't sound grief-stricken, she thought suddenly. In fact, his voice was cool and even. Almost containing a note of faint amusement.

She stared at him in confused disbelief as a small agony of shame began to uncurl inside her, commingled with anger, the spell which had enslaved her broken at last. And, if she was honest, only just in time.

Oh, God, she thought in shocked horror. What have I done? I couldn't have made it any easier for him if I'd tried.

He's totally sure of me now—and of himself...

But I should have stopped him—pushed him away, not waited for him to do it. What was I thinking of?

Except that she hadn't been thinking at all. Her reaction had been completely physical, born from the long months of deliberate starvation.

Nick, she realised, was glancing at his watch.

'In ten minutes I have an appointment with one of the tenants—Ted Radstock,' he went on, almost casually. 'And I'm sure you wouldn't want him to walk in and find us—together.'

By some superhuman effort she kept her own voice level. 'Knowing that, I'm surprised you—chose to detain me.'

'I'm not sure I did choose,' he said quietly. 'Kisses can be dangerous, Cally. With your mouth under mine, I—almost forgot everything else.'

'In any case,' she continued, as if he hadn't spoken, 'there was no way that I'd have allowed—things to go any further. A moment longer and I'd have been—out of here.'

His eyes narrowed. 'I had a very different impression.'

'You think I'd let you go on—mauling me like that—degrading me?' She gave a small scornful laugh. 'You flatter yourself. You—took me by surprise, that's all.'

'A marked improvement on never taking you at all.' His voice took on a new and dangerous softness.

As Cally turned to leave his hand shot out, clasping her wrist without gentleness. Stopping her in her tracks.

'What the hell are you doing?' She tried unavailingly to pull free.

'You seem to be running away again.' He picked up the phone from the desk, one-handed deftly punching in a number. 'I'm stopping you.'

'My major mistake,' Cally said huskily, trying to conceal her sudden trepidation. 'I should have kept running while I had the chance.'

'Probably.' He turned his attention to the phone, his voice charming. His grip on her arm like steel. 'Mrs Radstock? Good afternoon, it's Nick Tempest. Has Ted left yet, or could we possibly postpone our meeting until tomorrow? There's a matter here that requires my urgent attention.' He listened, smiling. 'That's fine, then. Tell him I'll call him.'

He put down the phone and looked back at her, the smiling charm wiped away, to be replaced by a stark purpose which terrified her.

Cally began to struggle in real earnest. 'Leave me alone,' she said, her voice high and breathless. 'You—you're hurting me. Let me go, damn you.'

'When I'm good and ready,' Nick said. 'And only when you've given me everything I want. Starting now. And how much it hurts is entirely up to you, darling.'

He reached for her, sweeping her up inexorably into his arms, and started with her towards the door.

'No.' She was desperate now, twisting in his unyielding hold as he carried her across the hall to the stairs. Then upwards. 'Nick—please—you're scaring me…'

His mouth was hard, his eyes like flint as he glanced down at her agonised face. 'Why? The incidence of virgins dying of shock during sex must be pretty low.'

They reached the bedroom and he shouldered his way in, striding across to the bed and dropping her almost contemptuously on to its yielding surface. Cally landed, winded and gasping, staring up at him as he discarded his shoes and socks, then pulled off his shirt and tossed it to one side, his hands going to the belt of his pants.

His voice was silk and ice. 'Take off your clothes, too, darling. Unless you want me to do it.'

No, she thought, in some paralysed corner of her mind. Not like this.

She struggled up on to her knees and paused, her hand going up to shield her suddenly dazzled eyes from the blaze of the early-evening sun as it streamed in through the long windows.

He noticed. 'Wait,' he said, swiftly and harshly. 'I'll draw the curtains.'

He crossed the room, outlined against the golden glare. Cally saw him reach up to drag the drapes together. Just as she'd watched him do a year ago, as she'd hidden in the shadows, her heart cracking open. Just as it was doing now…

She clasped her hands over her mouth to stifle the scream rising in her throat.

He came back to the bed, his footsteps slowing as he took in the rigid, kneeling figure, her eyes dilating in fright as she stared back at him over her locked hands.

Cally heard him sigh, the sound low and bitter as he sat down beside her, carefully maintaining, she realised, a small distance between them.

He said quietly, 'In God's name, don't look at me like that. I swear I didn't mean this to happen. But you get to me, Cally, like no other woman ever has or ever could.'

He reached out and gently took her hands from her mouth.

'Relax, darling. Lie down and let me hold you. I promise I won't hurt you. I won't do anything you don't want.'

Couldn't he see that she was hurting already—that she was falling apart, torn by jealousy and misery? she wondered wildly. Didn't he realise that this—kindness—this borrowed tenderness was almost harder to endure than anything that had gone before?

'Please—no.' She flung herself away from him. 'Don't you understand? I can't—I can't bear it.' The words were hers, but she didn't recognise the harsh strained voice that spoke them.

There was a silence, then he said evenly, 'How can you do this? How can you go from the brink of surrender to this—neurotic bloody resistance—in the space of a few minutes? And why issue the challenge in the first place if you can't live with the consequences?'

She didn't look at him. 'I—I thought I could. And I knew I had to try—for the sake of Gunners Wharf—for the people there. Because I was afraid that you'd cancel the agreement.'

The small hoarse whisper died away into another silence, more profound than the last.

Then Nick said softly, 'Ah, dear God.'

Cally felt him move—lift himself off the bed. Was aware of him collecting up the clothing he'd discarded.

When he spoke again, his tone was weary. 'Understand this, Cally. You're my wife, and I still have no intention of letting you go, until you've fulfilled the terms of our bargain. But I won't have my bed turned into a war zone either. Come to me when you're ready to make peace.'

'And if it never happens?' The breath caught in her throat.

'Ah, but it will,' he said. 'Out of sheer female curiosity, my sweet, if nothing else. And that's as good a starting point as any, I suppose.' He strolled to the door that led to his own room, and turned. 'And Gunners Wharf is still safe. You have my word.' His parting smile did not reach his eyes. 'I'll see you at dinner.'

Cally stayed where she was, unmoving. She wanted to cry, but she was beyond tears, her eyes and throat aching—burning.

Her grandfather had been so right, she thought wretchedly. She should have seen the danger for herself, and shunned Nick's company from the first. Instead, she'd allowed herself to be beguiled into falling in love with him. And he'd known. Known and been disconcerted by her naïve reaction to his casual befriending of a lonely girl.

He must have been, she thought stonily, because why else would he have distanced himself so deliberately in those weeks before she made herself go to London to look for work?

Yes, she'd needed a job, but one word, one sign from him, and she'd have stayed.

But not to be pitied by him, she thought with sudden fierceness. Nor to run the gamut of Adele's mocking looks and snide remarks.

She'd realised just in time that she was crying for the moon, and that she had to change her life. To accept that Nick was not just unattainable, but frankly embarrassed by the sheer transparency of her feelings for him.

And then her grandfather's illness had forced her premature return, and her chance of falling out of love with Nick had been lost for ever.

Looking down at the golden gleam of her new wedding ring, she wondered, as so many times before, at what point Nick had begun to seriously consider her for the role of his wife. She'd had a lot going for her, she thought bitterly. Young, gullible, and too besotted to realise he'd never actually said he loved her.

But then he hadn't needed to say very much at all. The devastating aftermath of her grandfather's death had delivered her to him, gift-wrapped. She'd only had to say yes, believing that her love had worked some kind of miracle. That he was her paladin. Her saviour. Until, of course, she had discovered the reality of their marriage.

And she risked suffering the same kind of humiliation all over again, if she allowed Nick to guess the truth about her headlong flight from him.

I went, she thought, because I couldn't bear to stay—to

know that I would never be all in all to him, as he was to me. And that I would always have to share him.

And nothing—nothing has changed.

Because no matter how hard I've tried, I've never managed to grind him out of my heart. Never given myself the chance to heal. Not yet, anyway.

But there'll be plenty of years ahead of me for that. A whole lifetime to learn to stop loving him. When all this is over…

She sat up slowly, pushing her hair back from her face.

All Nick required from her was the use of her body, she thought flatly, and in return maybe she could hope for his kindness, if nothing else.

Forget emotion, she told herself. Look on it as he does—just another business transaction. And do what you've been asked without argument.

Give him what he wants, even down to wearing your wedding dress at dinner tonight. And after dinner give him whatever else he wants…

And, bowing her head, Cally began at last to weep.

Cally fastened the last of the little silk-covered buttons and stepped back to examine her reflection in the long mirror. The dress seemed to have survived being discarded on the floor of the flat, but that was about as much as she could say.

I look like my own ghost, she thought, her mouth twisting. But that could be because of the bad memories.

She was almost tempted to change. Almost, but not quite.

For one thing, she couldn't afford to annoy Nick by contravening his express wish. For another, he had to be made to see that it didn't matter, she told herself, swallowing. That, as a garment, it held no particular meaning for her. And that nothing he could say or do to her during their time together could affect her. Whether that was true or not.

There were much bigger battles ahead of her, and she needed to save her strength for those. Unless she could persuade Nick to be reasonable, she might even find she was fighting for the upbringing—the future—of her own child…

She turned away, sinking her teeth into her lower lip. She wouldn't think about that now. It was pointless to torment herself over something that hadn't happened yet. That might never happen, she corrected herself. After all, there were no guarantees.

But, in that case, how long would it be before Nick accepted the inevitable and sent her on her way?

Nick...

He was dressing for dinner too. She'd heard him earlier, moving around in the other bedroom, and felt tension coil in her stomach. And that had to stop.

His presence—his absence—she had to learn to treat them both with equal indifference. But no one had said it would be easy.

She'd managed to bathe away the telltale signs of that terrible storm of tears. She still looked pale, but that was only natural under these impossible circumstances.

Now, she brushed her hair loose and shining on her shoulders, and applied a pale rose lustre to her lips. She'd even found a bottle of her favourite scent waiting for her on the dressing table.

He didn't forget much, she thought, with a sudden pang, as she sprayed a little on her skin.

She left it to the last minute to go downstairs. Nick was in the drawing room, standing by the open French windows, staring out into the darkness. As he turned to look at her Cally saw him stiffen, his whole attention arrested as if in shock.

Cally felt the hairs rise on the back of her neck in response to the sudden dangerous tension in the room.

Then, as if a cord had snapped, the moment passed. He said evenly, almost politely, 'You look very lovely.'

'Thank you.' Her tone was constricted. He looked a million dollars himself, she thought, in dinner jacket and black tie. The last time she'd seen him so formally dressed had been at the local hunt ball, when she'd waited hungrily, and in vain, for him to ask her to dance, and then gone home to cry bewildered tears into her pillow.

'There's champagne waiting for us,' he went on. 'The Thurstons have clearly decided this is an occasion.' He walked to the drinks table and lifted a bottle from its nest of ice, filling two flutes.

He handed her one, and lifted the other in salute. 'To life,' he said, and drank.

'To life,' Cally repeated nervously, as she raised the flute to her lips.

Dinner was special indeed—consommé, followed by a delicate fish mousse. Then roast duck in a sharp black cherry sauce, and Floating Islands pudding to complete the meal. Frank Thurston, a quiet, thin-faced man, waited at table, and his unobtrusive presence meant that conversation was limited to general subjects.

'Please tell Margaret that was magnificent.' Nick rose. 'If you'll bring the coffee to the drawing room, Frank, we won't need you again this evening.'

'Of course, sir. Thank you.' Frank Thurston was too well trained to look either knowing or indulgent, but Cally guessed he must have been sorely tempted.

She sat rigidly on the sofa, waiting for the tray to be brought in, then responding quietly as he wished them both goodnight and left.

There was a silence, then Nick said, 'Would you like some brandy?'

Cally shook her head. 'Just coffee will be fine.' She poured some of the richly fragrant brew into the cups and handed him one. 'You still take it black, I presume?'

'Yes.' He spoke with cool civility. 'Thank you.'

She sat sipping her coffee, glancing at him swiftly from under her lashes as he sat opposite her. She struggled to find the right words and, deciding there were none, thought she might as well be totally direct.

She replaced her cup on the tray and took a deep breath. 'Nick—there's something I need to say.'

'I'm listening.'

She kept her voice steady. 'I want you to know that I'm ready to—to keep the terms of our bargain.'

His brows lifted. 'Now?' There was a note of quiet incredulity in his voice. 'Tonight.'

She nodded convulsively.

There was another tingling silence. Nick got up, and went to the drinks table, pouring himself a brandy. He said, 'Cally, a couple of hours ago you were behaving as if I was the Antichrist. These about-turns of yours are making my head spin.'

She bit her lip. 'Yes, I—I'm sorry. I behaved rather badly, I know. I suppose I didn't like the sensation of being trapped all over again.'

He drank some brandy, the silvery eyes watching her over the rim of the goblet. 'Trapped—as in marriage to me?'

'Well—yes.' Cally managed a shrug. 'What can I say? I was young and scared, and didn't realise what I was doing. Now I just want to deal with my side of the bargain as soon as possible—get the whole thing over and done with—so I can be free to proceed with my own life.' She paused. 'Unless you've changed your mind, of course?'

'No,' he said slowly, his face and tone expressionless. 'I haven't done that.'

'Then—what do you think?'

He gave her a swift, brilliant smile, and finished his brandy. 'Sure,' he said. 'Why not? In your own classic phrase, let's get it over with.' He picked up the decanter. 'I'll join you presently, darling, after I've acquired a little more Dutch courage.'

She was taken aback. She'd expected some kind of reaction—that he would at least come to her—kiss her. The recent memory of being carried upstairs against his heart was still hot within her. But not, it seemed, for him.

She lifted her chin. 'I wouldn't have thought you needed it.'

'Ah,' Nick said softly. 'But then, you don't know me very well, do you, my sweet? At least, not yet. However, the night is young.'

Her throat tightened. 'Yes.' She turned, head high, and walked to the door, aware of his gaze following her.

'Cally.' His voice halted her. She looked back, feeling her heart quicken in something absurdly like hope.

'Don't have another change of heart and lock the door.' There was steel below the even tone. 'Because I would not find that amusing.'

'I've given my word.' She spoke curtly, fighting a disappointment she hardly understood. 'I won't go back on it now.'

He nodded, and turned back to the brandy.

And Cally went up the wide stairs into the darkness alone.

CHAPTER EIGHT

THE waiting seemed endless. As Cally paced restlessly up and down the big room, its details seemed to become indelibly printed on her mind.

Both sides of the bed had been turned down in readiness, presumably by Mrs Thurston, and shaded lamps burned on the night tables. The curtains moved softly in the faint breeze from the half-open window behind them.

Another of Cally's trousseau nightgowns—a charming piece of nonsense in flimsy white voile, with ribbon straps and a tiny bodice—had been fanned out across the bed. The one she'd worn the previous night had presumably been taken away for laundering. Cally wasn't at all sure she'd ever become accustomed to all this very personal service.

But then, as she swiftly reminded herself, she wouldn't have to. The situation was strictly temporary.

She realised suddenly that she was shivering, but not because she was cold. Some ten minutes ago she'd heard Nick walking quickly and quietly past the door and going into his own room, which meant that he would soon be joining her.

And she certainly didn't want to be found going round in circles like some pathetic caged animal. She went over to the dressing table and sat down, picking up her brush and beginning to smooth her hair with it. It was totally unnecessary—her hair was shining like silk already—but Cally was desperate for something to do—something to fill the empty time.

And she hoped, too, that the gentle, rhythmic movement of her hand and arm would help compose her. Because she badly needed to appear calm and in control. A woman who'd made an unwelcome but rational choice, and could deal with it.

Later, of course, as the night wore on, she could guarantee nothing.

She was no longer the eager girl of a year ago, living in a fool's paradise that promised her love and rapture in her husband's arms.

But recent experience had taught her the havoc his lightest touch could provoke in her senses. And Nick was well aware of it too, so any pretence at resistance or indifference would now be futile, she thought bleakly.

And tensed.

Because he was here. He had come into the room silently, barefoot and bare-legged in a black silk robe belted loosely round his waist, and was now standing behind her, watching her in the mirror.

'Not cowering under the sheets?' His voice was cool—almost derisive.

Cally shrugged. 'As you see,' she returned shortly.

'Are you planning to go to bed with your clothes on?'

She looked away. 'I—don't have any plans. I wasn't sure what you expected...' Her voice tailed away.

Nick leaned down and took the brush from her hand. 'I thought we agreed to get the whole tiresome business over and done with,' he said levelly. 'I mention it only because, if so, you can't spend the entire night, sitting there.'

'Of course not.' She hunched a shoulder again. 'I simply thought I'd better wait—a while.'

'Wait for what?' He sounded faintly amused. 'Do you want me to undress you? Because I'm more than willing.'

'No!' She sounded over-loud and defensive, she thought, swallowing, aware of the sudden thud of her heart. 'God—no.'

'Then you do it,' he said softly. 'And I'll watch.' He tossed the brush on to the dressing table and walked over to the bed, lounging across it with the air of a man preparing to enjoy himself. 'In your own time, of course.'

She got to her feet, her hands going mechanically to the buttons on the front of her dress, trying to fumble them free with fingers that shook.

I was fantasising about undoing them all—with my teeth.

Was it really only last night he'd said that? Or several lifetimes ago?

And did he really expect her to stand here and strip in front of him? Couldn't he realise that she'd never been even semi-naked in front of anyone before, least of all him, and this was a real ordeal for her? Or didn't he care that shyness and uncertainty were crucifying her?

'What's the matter, Cally?' he asked mockingly, as she hesitated. 'Not feeling quite so brave any more?'

She didn't look at him. 'No.' The word was little more than a breath.

There was a touch of impatience in his own sigh. He patted the bed beside him. 'Come here.'

She went slowly, sitting down on the edge of the mattress, her body rigid. Nick began to release the buttons from their loops, his fingers deft and oddly dispassionate, as if he was taking care not to touch the bare skin he was uncovering. When he'd finished, he reached for the nightgown and draped it over her arm.

'Get changed in the bathroom,' he directed quietly, to her utter astonishment. 'Longer than five minutes and I come to find you.'

Cally fled, hugging the flimsy folds in front of her like a shield. Which, of course, it wasn't, she realised, as soon as she slid it over her head, a few flurried moments later. The bodice's tiny ribbon-edged cups barely veiled her small breasts, and the long skirt was sheer when she was still, transparent when she moved.

But she'd bought it. Along with all the other pretty sexy things in her lingerie drawers that she'd hoped would please him. Because she'd wanted him. Wanted to turn him on.

She thought painfully, And, so help me, I still do...

She turned off the light and went back to the bedroom on reluctant bare feet.

Nick was in bed, his robe a pool of darkness on the floor.

Propped on one elbow, he watched her cross the room and slide nervously under the covers beside him.

'Admirably punctual,' he said softly.

Her throat was dry. 'Nick—please don't make fun of me.'

'I wasn't planning to.' He reached for her, drawing her to him, holding her close against the warmth of his body, her head pillowed on his shoulder. He said, 'Now, go to sleep.'

There was a short, amazed pause, then Cally said, 'I—I don't understand.'

'I hardly understand myself.' His mouth twisted. 'Except that it's been one hell of a bloody day, and hardly conducive to the fulfilment of passion, however one-sided,' he added with a touch of harshness. 'So, accustom yourself to sleeping with me, Cally, if nothing else. Get used to the idea of my arms being round you, because from now on that's how it's going to be.'

He switched off the lamp and the night enclosed them. Cally could feel the strong beat of his heart, the texture of his skin under her cheek, and felt longing stir within her.

In a way, this was her sweetest dream come true. In another, her worst nightmare, because wrapped in his arms like this she felt safe, and that was just another illusion to be discarded with the rest. Because with Nick there could be no safety—no comfort or lasting joy. It was all—ephemeral. And it was dangerous too, because when it ended it would be that much harder for her to detach herself and walk away.

When Cally opened her eyes, the room was just beginning to fill with pale grey light. She moved slowly, languidly, stretching a little, wondering what had woken her. She turned her head and saw Nick lying on his side, watching her.

He said, 'Good morning.'

'Is it?' She tried to see the small porcelain clock on the night table. 'It still seems very early.'

'It's dawn,' he said.

'Dawn?' Cally echoed incredulously. 'But I'm never awake this soon.'

He smiled at her. 'You can blame me for that. I decided to

wake you—like this.' He bent over her, brushing her lips gently with his. 'Do you have any objection?'

'No.' Her mouth framed the word but no sound would come.

'Good.' He pulled her into the curve of his body, his hand cupping her breast almost casually, as if he'd kissed her awake a thousand times before.

'It's the beginning of a new day,' he whispered, as she gasped. 'A perfect time to put everything in the past behind us, don't you think? To make a fresh start?'

He looked down into her widening eyes, then kissed her again, more deeply, coaxing her lips to part for him, allowing his tongue to tease hers delicately and sensuously.

In that moment she knew that the past couldn't simply be swept away as easily as he suggested. That it would always haunt her. Always have the power to hurt her. And the fact that his relationship with Vanessa Layton was by no means over would eventually inflict more pain upon her than she could stand.

She owed it to herself to fight him, she told herself desperately. To succumb without protest was a shameful thing.

At the same time she realised that it was not Nick she had to fight, but herself. She might be ashamed of her hunger for him, but she couldn't deny it, or hide it. And during their months apart it had grown into a famine.

Impossible, now, to resist the magic of his mouth moving on hers, inciting her to response. A little sigh rose in her throat as she yielded fully to the warm, persuasive pressure of his lips, holding nothing back, her hands going up to clasp his naked shoulders.

'Darling.' His voice was husky as he stroked the hair back from her face and trailed his fingers down the curve of her cheek and jaw to the vulnerable line of her throat. She felt her pulse leap uncontrollably as he caressed her. Felt a sharp, heated excitement uncoiling deep within her.

He kissed her again as his hands lingered, sliding under the ribbon straps of her gown and hooking them slowly down from her shoulders. The loosened fabric fell away, baring her to the waist.

Nick raised his head and looked down at her, the grey eyes brilliant and intense. He began to touch her again, to stroke the delicate scented mounds he'd uncovered, teasing their rosy crests with the tips of his fingers, urging them into hard, aching pleasure.

She moved restlessly, feeling her breathing change and catch in her throat as his lips followed the path of his hands. His mouth closed on her nipple, suckling it gently, tantalising it to sweet agony with the flicker of his tongue.

She heard herself moan softly, her body arching upwards in mute longing.

'Yes, darling,' he whispered. 'Yes.' He threw back the covers, tossing them to the end of the bed, and his hands moved down her body, freeing her completely from the folds of her gown. He lifted her, holding her close, letting her discover the abrasive sensuality of his nakedness against hers, as he kissed her again in a fierce, passionate demand that made few allowances for her comparative innocence.

It was as if he recognised the molten need within her, and knew that she did not wish to be spared.

She began to caress his shoulders, her hands urgent as they moved down the muscular length of his back. How long had she wondered how it would be to touch him—imagined how he might touch her?

And now every dream was becoming a physical, sensuous reality.

Cally was feverishly aware of his hand caressing her hip, moving inward to the flat plane of her stomach, then down in slow, languorous demand to the shadowy joining of her thighs. Found her small, startled cry stifled by his mouth as his fingers gently created a passage for this new intimacy—persuaded her, wordlessly, to accept this ultimate exploration of her secret, ungiven self.

She was lost immediately, her shocked body transported to a different dimension, twisting, almost sobbing under the clever, silken fingertips that were so expertly gliding on the moist inner heat of her at one moment, then, in the next, stroking the tiny hidden bud which was somehow the centre of all the pleasure that had ever been and bringing it to tumescent, irresistible arousal.

She wanted him to stop—she wanted him never to stop.

She realised dazedly that it was as if the last remaining knot of control inside her was being slowly, relentlessly undone. And there was nothing she could do to prevent it. To save herself.

As the final thread parted, she was aware of the first tremors of delight building inexorably within her, and cried out in a kind of fear. Then, suddenly, her whole being was shivering— convulsing in endless sensations of almost agonised rapture. And there was no longer any room for fear.

She could hear herself moaning. Felt each blissful pulsation reverberating in every nerve-ending, every drop of blood that she possessed.

At last, the exquisite savagery tearing her apart began to fade, and as she lay stunned and helpless with delight, her body totally relaxed in the final echoes of rapture, Nick began gently to ease his way into her.

Gasping, she looked up into his taut, absorbed face. The grey eyes were pools of silver as they met hers.

'Am I hurting you?' His voice was quiet, but urgent, and she turned her head in instant negation, still holding his gaze, astonished that it should all seem so simple, and so right. Knowing herself finally claimed, and totally possessed. Amazed at her own capacity to welcome and absorb such awesome strength and potency.

Some undreamed-of female instinct told her to lift her legs and wrap them round his hips, enfolding him, drawing him into her more deeply, and she heard him groan softly in response as he began to move, his rhythm slow and powerful at first, then increasing. And Cally moved with him, her hands grasping his sweat-slicked shoulders, blindly mirroring every driving male thrust.

He said hoarsely, 'Darling—my sweet angel.' She heard the sudden rasp of his changed breathing, then his body shuddered scaldingly into hers.

The silence that followed was profound—endless. She wondered if he'd fallen asleep. But eventually he moved, lifting himself away from her.

He said softly, 'Are you all right?' and she nodded jerkily, but she wasn't sure that it was true. She'd just had her first experience of sex, and it had been wholly sensational—the stuff that delirium was made of. But Nick would have made sure of that, she told herself, biting her lip. After all, he had a reputation to maintain.

Lovemaking, she thought numbly, with no pretence at love.

Not that she could blame him. She'd hardly been a challenge, she derided herself bleakly, remembering Adele's jibe. More a total push-over.

Now she felt strangely lost, and was suddenly aware that tears were not far away, tightening her throat and tingling behind her eyelids. Because for him it had simply been a means to an end, with any attendant pleasure merely a bonus. And one day she would be left with only the memory of that pleasure to haunt her—hurt her. Along with so much else, she thought with desolation.

'Haven't you anything to say?' Nick's tone was lazy as he reached out a long arm and scooped her towards him.

The conqueror, Cally thought. Reviewing yet another triumph. She pulled away a little.

She said in a small, quiet voice, 'If you've finished with me, I thought I'd have a bath.'

'I'll get some champagne,' he said softly. 'And we'll take one together. During which we'll discuss whether or not I've finished with you.'

She could hear the smile in his voice and resented it. How many women did he need, begging for his favours? she asked herself wildly. He'd made her behave like—like an animal.

Aloud, she said, 'I think I'd prefer to be on my own.'

There was a pause. 'Cally,' he said, 'what's the matter?'

She rolled away, presenting him with her back. 'What do you want to hear?' she asked tautly. 'The sex was amazing—mind-blowing. On a wow factor of ten. All those things. Or would you prefer a round of applause?'

There was another silence, this one frankly ominous. Then, 'Oh, I think any plaudits should come from me,' he drawled. 'You clearly have a great natural talent, sweetheart, which I look forward to exploiting. And bloody soon too.'

'That may not be necessary,' she said. 'After all, I might have beginner's luck and already be pregnant.'

'It's possible,' he said.

'So,' she added, 'we'll just have to—wait and see.'

'An interesting suggestion,' Nick said, too pleasantly. 'But I've waited long enough. Besides, we can't guarantee to reach the target first time around, and I would hate to think I'd taken all that trouble just to be disappointed.'

Every word bit, and Cally found herself wincing inwardly.

She said, 'Meaning?'

'Meaning,' he said icily, 'that you'll continue to share a bed with me, with all that entails, until that possibility you mentioned becomes a bloody certainty.'

He swung himself off the bed, reaching down for his robe. 'And now take your bath, or your shower. Scrub yourself all over with carbolic, if you think it will help. You won't keep me away.'

She made herself turn—look up at him. 'Nick—please...'

'Yes,' he said. 'I do please. I want you, Cally, and I intend to have you whenever and however I desire.' His smile was like the lash of a whip laid across her shaking body. 'You see, my sweet, you still have a lot to learn, and I'm going to enjoy teaching you. How you feel about it is entirely up to you.'

He strode over to the communicating door, and went out, slamming it behind him. Cally was left staring after him, one hand pressed to her mouth. She'd gone too far, and she knew it, and wished the words left unsaid.

She'd spoken out of a kind of bravado, in a belated effort

to protect herself. To justify, if it was possible, her abandoned, passionate surrender to him.

Why hadn't she obeyed her first instinct and curled up in his arms to bask in their mutual satiation? she wondered despairingly. Instead, she'd tried to salvage some remnants of pride, and it had rebounded on her badly.

She was almost tempted to follow him, but what could she say without betraying all those things that must not be said?

Things like—I love you, Cally thought, and wanted to weep.

It was beginning to look like rain. The July morning had started brightly, but now grey clouds were massing in the west and a chill wind had risen, sighing among the trees in the Home Wood.

Cally supposed she should turn back to the Hall. Baz hated wet weather, and she'd come out without even a jacket for protection. But this couple of hours each day, when she wandered round the countryside on Baz's amiable, elderly back, was her own personal time, when she could get away, just for a while, from the burden of being Lady Tempest. The downside, of course, was that she also found herself alone with her increasingly unhappy thoughts. And problems that would not go away.

It was as if her life with Nick was split into two separate and distinct halves, proceeding on parallel lines, but never touching.

There was the daytime life where, among other things, she was being gently inducted by Frank and Margaret into the efficient running of the Hall. Where she picked flowers from the garden and arranged them in vases and bowls. Where she entertained visitors to tea, some of them genuinely friendly, others merely curious to take a look at Sir Nicholas's errant bride. Where she dealt with correspondence with the help of Janette from the village, a former City secretary now living in rural bliss with her husband and young family.

She found herself being invited to join local clubs and so-

cieties, and to serve on the committee for the annual charity
fête, which was always held in the Hall's grounds.

On Nick's instructions, she sent out invitations to lunch and
dinner parties, and weekend guests, and steeled herself to play
hostess—with, she'd come to realise, surprising success.

On the down side, Adele was still occupying the Dower
House, and finding excuses to come up to the Hall too regularly
to suit Cally, who was usually left shaking with anger after her
visits. But without an electric fence it seemed impossible to
keep her out.

And Cally was powerless to prevent Adele's knife slipping
beneath her ribs either.

'You're looking tired, my pet,' she'd remarked solicitously
only the previous day, encountering Cally in the garden on her
way up from the stables. 'But don't worry. I hear on the village
grapevine that Vanessa Layton's coming back this week, so
Nick will soon have an alternative outlet for all that incredible
masculine energy.'

And she drifted off, leaving Cally to stare after her with
murder in her heart.

But at least she knew now, and could be on her guard, she
told herself. Although there was little she could do about the
situation. Nick, as he'd demonstrated with chilling force over
the past weeks, was his own man, and would do precisely as
he wished.

Adele, she thought, sighing, vicious little jibes notwithstand-
ing, was the very least of her difficulties. Her relationship with
Nick was the problem that overrode all others, and filled her
mind and heart, waking or sleeping. Or rather, the lack of it.

The harsh words they'd exchanged a few weeks before had
been their last real conversation, she acknowledged miserably.
When he was at the Hall they met at mealtimes, which were
conducted in silence, apart from a few polite and formal ex-
changes.

Probably, Cally admitted, for the look of the thing. Although
she suspected the Thurstons were already aware that the atmo-
sphere could be cut with a knife most of the time.

Each morning Nick went for an early-morning ride on Maestro, his chestnut gelding, before leaving for the day, but it was never suggested that Cally should join him, and he avoided the routes she used with Baz.

'Just as well,' Lorna had commented cheerfully, when Cally had diffidently raised the subject. 'He's a terrific rider, and he really pushes Maestro.' She laughed. 'I have a job to keep up with him on a young horse, so poor old Baz wouldn't get a look-in—although he might try, and it wouldn't be good for him.'

'No.' Cally had forced a smile. 'No, of course not.'

At other times he worked in his study, and it was made clear he was not to be interrupted.

He was treating her much like an employee, she thought. There'd been a time when she'd believed this could be a way for her to cope. But she'd been wrong.

And the pattern was repeated on the occasions when she was required to accompany him to London, to attend formal dinners in the City and other social events. Her wardrobe, most of it selected under Nick's stringent supervision, had expanded dramatically to meet these new demands, and she had the beginnings of an astonishing jewellery collection to match.

She could not, of course, question his generosity, which was unfailing, but then he'd made it clear he expected her to do him credit in public.

So the clothing and jewels were merely props, she thought, to be handed back when her run-of-the-play contract ended. But what else could she expect?

In public, Nick was the most quietly charming and attentive husband any young wife could wish. And only Cally knew of his cool aloofness when they were alone together.

Except at night…

She felt her whole body shiver, and Baz, as if sensing her sudden restlessness, flung up his head and whinnied. She murmured to him, running a soothing hand down his neck.

Nick had meant every word he'd said before they'd parted in that pale dawn, she thought wretchedly. They had not spent a single night apart since, even though the demands of work took him on punishing trips all over the country and he often returned very late, almost grey with tiredness. Those were the times when he simply turned his back and slept, while she lay beside him, staring into the darkness, aware of an ever-deepening sense of isolation.

At such moments Cally yearned to reach out to him and draw him close. To let him sleep away his exhaustion in her arms, his head pillowed on her body. But she had never dared initiate such a move, in case she was rebuffed.

She had learned her lesson on the evening they'd been scheduled to attend a banquet in London. Cally had worn a new dress in taffeta, long-sleeved with a full skirt and scooped neck, the colour of autumn leaves. It had been Nick's choice, and she'd had to admit that the shade complemented her newly highlighted hair and lent a sheen and glow to her pale, creamy skin.

She'd opened her jewellery case, in search of the exquisite diamond necklace which had been his first gift to her, but he'd stopped her abruptly. Instead, he'd fastened round her neck an antique topaz pendant, set in tiny pearls. She'd stared at it, the breath catching in her throat, aware that it seemed somehow a much more personal gift than diamonds, however lovely.

She'd put up a hand to touch it in delight, wondering if it could be a slender sign of hope. Then, stammering, 'It's—so beautiful,' she'd swung round impulsively to kiss him, only to have him turn his head swiftly, so that her lips touched his cheek instead of his mouth. Her face flaming in humiliation, she'd managed to add a stilted, 'Thank you,' then turned away, and begun hurriedly, with shaking hands, to fill her evening purse.

Since then she hadn't risked anything that could be construed as an advance, even if she was aching for him, as she so often did.

Although she could not claim she was neglected, she thought, her mouth twisting wryly. The nights when he did not make love to her were rare indeed.

But was it really 'making love'? she asked herself. Was that really how to describe that web of silken carnality that he'd spun around her so skilfully, to keep her trapped and enthralled? Because, apart from that first unforgotten time, when he'd taken her with such apparent tenderness and understanding, it all seemed curiously soulless.

A demonstration of high-art sexual technique, she thought, rather than uncontrollable passion. A master-class in which he treated her body as some finely toned instrument solely designed for pleasure, and in which her ability to respond seemed to be taken to fresh limits each time, as he built sensation on sensation.

And there was nothing she could do about it except submit to the promised rapture and, she supposed, be thankful.

Once—just once—ashamed of her unthinking, abandoned response, wanting to make him see her as a woman and not merely a sex-object, she'd tried to resist. Only to have Nick take her to the brink of climax over and over again, holding her there relentlessly, until she implored him for her release, the hoarse, uneven words torn from her throat.

Since then, when he reached for her she went silently and willingly into his arms, her body coming to swift, burning life under the caress of his hands and mouth.

After all, she thought with sadness, it was all she had of him. Because afterwards there was nothing. Even though she longed for him to hold her until she fell asleep, he invariably turned away without a word.

But she could hardly blame him for that, she acknowledged, sighing. Wasn't that exactly what she'd done to him that first morning? Oh, God, what a fool she'd been.

She should have forgotten her pride and gone into his arms, she told herself. Taken the risk. Let him see then that she wanted more than just physical gratification. But now it was all too late.

Because she was pregnant. She was sure of it. Her normally reliable monthly cycle had gone into total abeyance. She had just missed a second period, she'd been sick more than once in the past fortnight, so all she needed was the doctor's confirmation.

And Nick must be well aware of it. She'd seen a grim expression on his face more than once in recent days. Perhaps he was now regretting the bargain he'd inflicted on her. Wondering, maybe, how he was going to break the news to his mistress that his wife was pregnant, she thought with pain.

Yet he'd said nothing—waiting, she supposed, for her to speak first. To admit she'd fulfilled the cold-blooded remit she'd been given and was indeed carrying his child.

So what on earth was making her hesitate? Why didn't she say what needed to be said?

Because, according to the terms we agreed, I know it's the beginning of the end, she thought. Once I actually admit that I'm having a baby, I've taken the first step towards dissolving the marriage.

And I don't know what will happen afterwards.

Yes, that was the stumbling block. Somehow, she knew, she had to talk to Nick—discover what his long-term intentions were. 'Joint custody—at first,' he'd told her. And, 'Any lasting decision can be made later.'

Since she'd realised her condition, those words had been preying on her mind. Scaring her. Because there was no legal agreement between them about the baby's future. Nothing in writing.

And supposing Nick decided he wanted sole custody, and treated her as if she was a single mother giving her baby up for adoption? What would she do then?

Surely he couldn't, she thought, her stomach churning uneasily. He wouldn't…

After all, she reminded herself painfully, they were hardly more than two strangers who met in bed. There was no real marriage between them. No sign of affection or friendship to prompt her to hope that he would treat her well. She'd done as she'd been asked, he might tell her, and was now free to go.

Leaving her baby to be brought up by other strangers. Or

even Vanessa Layton, Nick's childless mistress. Once his unwanted wife had been dismissed and divorced, he'd be free to move her in. Cally shuddered away from the thought.

A year ago she'd thought her heart was broken. But the prospect ahead of her could be infinitely worse than anything she'd suffered then. And she was frightened to confront him in case her worst fears were confirmed and she found herself entering the New Year in total isolation, faced with a long and agonising struggle for the right to bring up her own child, or even be allowed proper access.

I told Nick I wanted to be set free, she reminded herself unhappily. *That I wanted to get on with my life without hindrance. I insisted on it.*

Beware what you wish for, someone had said once. *Because it might come true.*

She sighed, and gave an apprehensive look at the sky as a faint rumble of thunder sounded over the far hills.

'Time to go home, lovely,' she told Baz, whose ears were suddenly pricked attentively. And then she heard what he must have done—the distressed and muffled yapping of a dog in the distance. 'But we'll go and look first,' she added, clicking her tongue to quicken his gait.

She left the bridleway, and rode through the trees, bent low in the saddle to avoid overhanging branches, listening intently for the increasingly frantic barking and whimpering.

Eventually, in a small clearing, she found the dog—or his rear portion anyway. It was protruding from an overgrown bank, and Cally guessed that the animal had gone into a hole after a rabbit and had earth and stones collapse on him, so that he couldn't move forwards or back.

She slid down from Baz and looped his reins over a convenient bush. It didn't take long to shift the debris and free the dog, a Jack Russell, who immediately repaid her by nipping her hand.

'Not nice,' Cally told him gently. 'But I know what it's like to be trapped and frightened, so I forgive you.'

The name on his collar tag was unfamiliar, and the telephone code wasn't local.

'But you must belong to someone,' Cally mused, winding her hankie round her hand. She tucked the now shivering and subdued dog under her arm, and began to lead Baz towards the edge of the wood and the road beyond.

As they came out from the trees she heard a shrill whistle, and a voice call 'Tinker!' An elderly man came round the corner. He was using a stick, and walking with a pronounced limp, but his thin, anxious face lit up when he saw Cally and her suddenly wriggling burden.

'Tinker, you little devil. My dear young lady, I can't thank you enough. Where did you find him?'

'He'd managed to get stuck in a rabbit hole, but I was able to dig him out.' Cally handed the dog over, and saw his leash securely attached to his collar.

'At home he's no trouble at all,' the man said, sighing. 'But I'm afraid whenever I bring him away he invariably runs off at some point. And I've just had a hip replacement, so I can't chase him as I once did.' The faded blue eyes sharpened. 'My dear, your hand—did he do that?'

'Yes,' Cally admitted. 'But it's not that bad. He barely broke the skin, and he was in an awful state.'

'I'm staying not far from here.' His voice was firm. 'You must let me disinfect the cut and put on a plaster. And I think a cup of tea is indicated too.'

'Really, there's no need,' she began, but he raised a silencing hand.

'I insist. Besides, I think we need to get indoors before we become soaked. It really isn't far, and there's a shortcut across this field. My name's Geoffrey Miller,' he went on, as he opened the gate for them. 'And this, of course, is Tinker the Terrible.'

'And I'm Caroline Maitland.' Was that a Freudian slip? Cally wondered, realising she'd given her maiden name. 'And I think Tinker and I met before,' she added. 'He once gate-crashed a picnic I was at.'

Her companion groaned. 'Two things draw him like magnets—food and rabbits. I'll have to start keeping him on a lead while I'm here.'

'Are you on holiday?' Cally enquired, as the first heavy spots of rain began to fall.

'Not quite. I'm spending a few weeks with my daughter. Convincing her that I'm going to be able to manage on my own.' He shook his head wryly. 'She does worry about me, bless her. And she has so much else to cope with. She's spent her life recently running between two hospitals. Visiting me in the mornings, and spending the afternoons with her husband. She's so brave and hopeful, but I suspect it's useless.'

'Oh.' Cally digested this. 'Is he seriously ill?'

'He's in a coma, after a bad road accident just over two years ago. At first it was thought he'd come out of it, then tests revealed serious brain damage. But she won't give up. She talks to him, reads and plays music, but there's no response.' He sighed. 'So far she's refused to allow the life-support to be switched off, but I'm afraid that can only be a matter of time.'

'That's terrible,' Cally said quietly. Oh God, she thought, if that was Nick lying unconscious and helpless, wouldn't I do the same? Keep vigil beside him, praying for a miracle? Try to keep the flame alive, even when hope is gone?

'Nearly there,' he announced, as they came through another gate and down on to a lane. And suddenly, like the flash of lightning that had just split the sky above them, Cally realised exactly where she was heading. And why she couldn't go a step further.

Her footsteps faltered as she tried desperately to think of an excuse, and the patient Baz tossed his head in surprise.

'And there's my daughter, waiting at the gate now,' Geoffrey Miller announced with a smile. He waved his stick jovially. 'We're safe and sound, Vanessa,' he called. 'And look, I've brought a visitor.'

And, with a roar of thunder, the heavens opened.

CHAPTER NINE

She would have given anything to fling herself on Baz's back and ride away, leaping hedges, ditches and five-barred gates to escape from this hideous situation.

It was small consolation to observe that Vanessa Layton, the woman she'd last seen held close in Nick's arms, seemed equally dismayed.

Cally felt her colour rise. She said, 'I think it would be better if I made for home. I don't want to intrude.'

'In this rain? Utter nonsense,' Geoffrey Miller told her severely. 'You'll catch pneumonia.' He addressed his daughter. 'There'll be room for the horse in the lean-to at the side, won't there, darling.'

Vanessa Layton appeared to come out of her trance. 'Yes—yes, of course.' She had a quiet, musical voice, currently a little strained. Seen at closer quarters, her face held traces of a sadness which by no means detracted from her beauty. 'If you'll show Lady Tempest where everything is, I'll get some water.'

'Tempest?' he queried. 'Isn't that the name of your landlord, Vanessa?' He gave Cally a puzzled look. 'I thought you said Maitland.'

Cally's flush deepened. 'That's my maiden name,' she admitted. 'I'm not very used to being married yet.'

And thought she saw Vanessa Layton's mouth tighten as she turned away.

The lean-to was more commonly used as a log store, but it was dry, and Baz seemed content with it.

'I'm going to find a dressing for your hand, and make some tea,' Mr Miller said cheerfully. 'Come to the house when you're ready.'

How could she ever be ready for a situation like this? Cally wondered, swallowing, as she loosened Baz's girths. As she did so, she saw Vanessa Layton approaching, carrying a striped golf umbrella, with the promised pail of water in her other hand.

Cally unconsciously straightened her shoulders. She said, 'I'm sorry about this. Please believe it wasn't intentional.'

The other woman shrugged, placing the pail where Baz could reach it. 'Dad has explained. But I suppose it was inevitable that we would meet eventually.' Her voice was cold. 'I've rung the Hall and told them you were caught by the storm,' she added reluctantly. 'They're sending a car for you, and the groom is bringing over the horsebox.'

'Thank you—that's very kind.' Also surreal, thought Cally.

'Don't mention it,' Vanessa Layton said curtly. 'I'm sure you don't want to spend any more time here than you have to.'

Cally lifted her chin. 'No,' she said. 'I don't.'

There was a brief nod, then the older woman said swiftly, almost jerkily, 'But there is something I have to ask you—a favour. As you heard, Dad believes Nick and myself are just—landlord and tenant. He has no idea there's another relationship, and he—he can't know. He must never know. So—please—I beg you—don't say anything about it to him.'

'Why?' Cally clenched her hands in the pockets of her jeans, anger rising within her. She didn't want to find herself in any kind of collusion with Nick's mistress. She owed her nothing, she thought. Nothing. 'Would it damage your perfect daughter image in his eyes?'

Vanessa Layton said quietly, 'It would totally destroy him.'

There was a taut silence.

A voice inside Cally's head was screaming *And what about me? I've been destroyed too—or doesn't that count?*

And then she remembered the kind, concerned, uncomprehending face, and sighed, swiftly and restlessly. Yes, she thought. Geoffrey Miller clearly believed in his daughter as the selfless, devoted wife to her dying husband. Why should his illusions be shattered, as hers had been, by discovering that when she wasn't playing Florence Nightingale, she was involved in a sordid affair with a married man?

'Don't worry,' she tossed back at her antagonist, her tone edged with contempt. 'Your secret is safe with me.' *But possibly not with Adele,* she added silently. However, that was not her problem. And she saw no reason to mention it. 'Actually, I don't find it important enough to mention,' she added stonily.

'Thank you.' Vanessa Layton's own tone was short. 'The tea should be ready by now, if you'd like to come indoors. But be careful on the cobbles. They get slippery in the rain.' She paused. 'And you certainly don't want to risk a fall, not at this particular time. In fact, you probably shouldn't be riding.'

Cally stopped dead, her whole body stiffening, her eyes blazing. Oh, God, she thought. Oh, dear God—no... He not only knows, but he's told her—*he's told her.*

Cally's voice shook. 'You have no right—no right at all to intrude into my personal circumstances. Or comment. And if ever I should want your damned advice, I'll ask for it. But don't hold your breath.'

Vanessa Layton threw back her head. 'Don't you even care that you're having Nick's child?' she demanded.

'Jealous, Mrs Layton?' The horrible, unforgivable words were out before she could stop herself. 'Wishing that it was your pregnancy instead?'

The pain in the other woman's eyes almost made her flinch. She said, too evenly, 'That will never be possible, Lady Tempest, as I'm sure you already know. And now my—my father is waiting to attend to your hand.'

While other wounds are left to bleed on both sides, Cally thought, hating herself.

Inside the cottage, the rooms were on the small side, with low ceilings, but light paint on the walls and pale floor coverings and fabrics had created a sense of space that was elegant and peaceful.

But what did I expect? Cally asked herself. The woman had trained in interior design. And Nick's London apartment had the same cool, uncluttered look, she thought, biting her lip. She could remember thinking how lovely it was—until she'd recalled exactly who was responsible for it.

There was a tray of tea and a plate of biscuits ready on a side table, and Geoffrey Miller was waiting with hot water, antiseptic cream, and a box of plasters.

'Oh, please, it's really nothing.' Cally tried to withdraw her hand. She was aware there was no sound from upstairs, where Vanessa Layton had gone after quietly excusing herself.

But he was firm. 'Better to be safe than sorry about these things. And I don't want Vanessa to be evicted for harbouring a dangerous dog.'

'As you see, butter wouldn't melt in his mouth.' In spite of herself, Cally found she was smiling as the sinner sat up in front of her, urgently waving his paws. 'But I'm sure a biscuit would.'

'You have a very forgiving nature, my dear.' Geoffrey Miller said as he carefully adjusted the strip of plaster.

All evidence to the contrary, Cally thought bleakly, as she broke off a piece of shortcake and threw it to Tinker, who leapt joyfully and caught it. By dint of keeping him supplied, she was able to pretend she was eating, and managed to swallow most of her cup of tea before she heard the arrival of the car outside.

'That sounds like my lift.' She rose hurriedly. 'Thank you for taking care of me, Mr Miller.'

'It's been my pleasure.' He hesitated. 'I'm sorry you didn't get more of a chance to talk to Vanessa. I think she's feeling the strain of her morning's visit. But there'll be other times, I'm sure. And I think the rain has stopped.'

He opened the front door as he spoke. Cally had expected that Frank or Margaret would come for her. Instead, she was confronted by the sight of Nick approaching up the path—but he was not alone, she realised, anger and hurt twisting inside her.

Because somehow Vanessa was no longer upstairs, but walking beside him, her voice soft and rapid, as he listened, head bent towards her.

The sight of them together was suddenly a torment impossible to bear, and Cally gasped, her head swimming, nausea hot and acrid in her throat.

'My dear child, you're ill.' Geoffrey Miller's hand grasped her arm. He raised his voice. 'Help me, would you? Lady Tempest is fainting.'

Then Nick was there, his arm like a ring of steel round her swaying body, his voice harsh. 'Let me take her. She needs to get home and rest, that's all.'

She heard herself say, 'Please—I'm all right—I'm fine,' as she tried to free herself and stand straight, but his grip simply tightened inexorably.

'Whatever,' he said curtly. 'You're coming with me, Cally, and you're coming now.'

She was put into the passenger seat of the car, and sat fumbling with the seatbelt while Nick strode round to the driver's side, almost flinging himself behind the wheel. With an exclamation of impatience, he took the buckle from her unsteady fingers and slotted it home.

'Thank you.' Cally took a deep breath. 'You must be wondering…'

'Wondering?' His voice cut across her stumbling words. He was, she realised, molten with rage. 'I come home to be informed that my pregnant wife is wandering round the countryside in a thunderstorm on the back of an elderly horse with a heart problem, and that you were due back an hour before. It takes a phone call from a neighbour to tell me where you are.'

A neighbour, she thought. *A neighbour…*

Nick hit the steering wheel with his clenched fist. 'Well, that stops now, Cally. From now on you take your exercise on your own two feet.' He added grimly, 'Do I make myself clear?'

'I was perfectly safe,' she protested. 'Baz isn't bothered by storms.'

'But he's still old,' Nick said unanswerably. 'If he got sick and went down you could be injured. I won't let you take that risk.' He started the car and drove up the lane. Cally did not look back to see if their departure was being observed.

She took a deep breath. 'As a matter of interest, why have you come home? You're supposed to be at meetings in London all day.'

'I postponed them,' he said brusquely. 'My mother's arrived.'

Cally sat up. 'But she wasn't due for another two weeks,' she said, aware that her stomach was churning again.

He shrugged a shoulder. 'She simply decided to get an earlier plane. She telephoned from Heathrow this morning, so I rang to warn you that I was bringing her down, but you weren't around.'

She looked down at her hands, knotted together in her lap. 'I'm sure Margaret was able to fill the breach.'

'Of course,' he said. 'But that doesn't let you off the hook, sweetheart. What the hell did you think you were doing?'

'I—I didn't go to the cottage deliberately,' she said in a low voice. 'It was all a chapter of accidents. I rescued Mr Miller's dog, and got bitten, and he insisted I go back with him to have my hand seen to and shelter from the rain.' She paused. 'But I wasn't snooping.'

'Did I suggest that you were?' Nick pulled the car over to the side of the road and stopped on the verge. He said, more gently, 'Cally, we can't go on like this. There are things that need to be said, particularly now.' His mouth tightened. 'And I need to tell you—explain about Vanessa. I should have done it long ago.'

'There's no need.' It hurt to breathe, let alone speak. 'Because I already know the whole story.'

His brows snapped together in disbelief. '*She* told you?'

'No,' she said. 'No, I knew—before.'

'I don't believe it,' Nick said, after a pause. 'How could you? We've always been so careful...' He stopped, apparently giving himself a mental shake. 'So where did you hear it?'

She said wearily, 'From Adele, naturally. Who else? She implied it was common gossip,' she added, after an uncertain pause. She'd opened up a can of worms here, she realised nervously. His next question was bound to be, Is that why you left me? And she wasn't sure she could survive the kind of revelations that were bound to follow.

'Adele,' he said quietly. 'My God—Adele. It beggars belief. But it will have to be dealt with. I've also left that too long.' He paused. 'So what did you talk about with Vanessa?'

She managed a shrug. 'Not a great deal. She gave me some unwanted advice, then asked me not to mention your relationship with her to her father.'

He looked at her, his brows raised. 'And you agreed?'

'Why not?' She braced herself. 'It's really of no concern or interest to me. After all, I'm unlikely to meet Mrs Layton again, or her father.'

He said carefully, 'I hoped you might be a little more understanding. She's been having a really bad time of late.'

'So her father said,' Cally said coldly. 'According to him, she's practically a saint. The perfect wife.'

'I think she was,' Nick returned with equal *froideur*. 'Until that motorway pile-up intervened. Now she's in limbo.'

No, Cally thought, with sudden violence. She has you. I'm the one in limbo!

Aloud, she said, 'Perhaps we should go. Your mother will be waiting.'

'My mother is resting after a hellish flight,' he returned. 'And there are still matters we need to deal with, especially as we're talking about Vanessa.'

'Don't tell me,' Cally said with bitter irony. 'You and the tenant of Southwood Cottage are simply good friends?'

'It would be better if you could refrain from mentioning her at all.' He hesitated. 'In fact, that's essential.'

'You mean your mother still has illusions?' Cally shrugged again. 'But, what the hell? Consider it done. Was there anything else?'

'A few things come to mind,' Nick said slowly. 'Such as when were you going to share your precious secret with me— tell me you were having my baby? Or did you hope it would all go away and you'd wake up one morning to find it was all a bad dream?'

Cally flushed. 'Naturally before I said anything I wanted to be absolutely sure.'

'Which symptoms would have convinced you?' Nick asked grimly. 'Actually going into labour?'

Her colour deepened. 'Kindly don't laugh at me.'

'Believe me,' he said, 'I've never felt less like laughing in my entire life.'

'Anyway, it wasn't much of a secret, because you've known all along,' she said tautly. 'You even told your—your Mrs Layton. And I expect you broke the news to your mother, too, and that's why she's arrived early.'

'It's her first grandchild,' he said. 'She's bound to be delighted. And she'll expect us to be thrilled too, so your performance as devoted wife will need to be stepped up a notch.'

'Don't worry,' Cally returned, 'I'm becoming quite expert at fooling people.'

Nick's smile was swift and hard. 'How very true.'

'Perhaps you need a little practice, too,' she said. 'For someone who's got exactly what he wanted, you're hardly jumping for joy.'

'I felt you might regard such displays as tactless.'

'Why?' She didn't look at him. 'After all, I'll soon be getting what I want too.'

'Of course,' he said sardonically. 'I almost forgot. So, shall we behave like prospective parents, Cally? Shall we hold each other and cry with happiness? Shall we argue about whether we're having a girl or a boy, and make lists of names and bicker over them? Then get serious and discuss schools and universities, and future careers for the tiny thing growing inside you?' He took her chin, making her face him, the silvery eyes glittering like ice. 'Shall I make sure, my sweet wife, that not even a breeze blows on you too roughly over the next seven months?'

If only, her heart cried out to him. *Oh, God, if only...*

And she suddenly had an image of Vanessa Layton's face, smiling faintly. An image that would haunt her, she knew, through all the remaining days she spent with Nick.

Her stomach began to churn again, in rejection and jealousy, and there were tears, hot and heavy, in her chest. Her voice sounded thick as she jerked her head away, scared of what he might read in her eyes. 'Or shall we just congratulate each other on a successful deal?'

She undid her seatbelt and fumbled for the door handle. 'And now, if you'll excuse me, I'm going to be sick.'

The doctor that Nick had insisted on calling was a woman, slim and blonde, in her early thirties, who was quick to be reassuring.

'No, there's no need for you to be wrapped in cotton wool, but your husband is right to err on the side of caution. Basically you seem very well, Lady Tempest, if a little tense, so enjoy some pampering, and I'll see you next week for the necessary tests and paperwork.' She paused. 'I don't know if Sir Nicholas is planning for you to have the baby in London, but I can assure you that the hospital at Clayminster has an excellent obstetric unit. In fact, I can personally recommend it.'

She got to her feet. 'One more thing. For the next few weeks, it might be as well to put marital relations on hold—just to be on the safe side.'

'Yes,' Cally said woodenly. 'Of course.'

'I realise this won't be easy, as you haven't been married very long, but you can resume around the fourth month,' Dr Hanson went on. Her smile had an engaging twinkle. 'Some people find it gets even better.'

She picked up her bag. 'By the way, your husband was obviously concerned when, as he was bringing you home earlier, you began to cry and couldn't stop. But I explained that hormonal changes might well make you a little weepy and grouchy at first.'

Cally flushed. She said, with a touch of constraint, 'I think it was more the humiliation of having him hold my head while I threw up in front of him at the side of the road.'

'I think he took it all in his stride.' The doctor gave her a sympathetic look. 'After all, it's his baby too. I was sick with both my boys, but it stopped in the third month, thank heaven. Unless you're very unlucky, you'll probably find the same.'

Cally forced a smile. 'I'll just have to hope for the best.'

She was lying back against the pillows, gazing listlessly into space, a few minutes later when Nick came in.

He sat down on the edge of the bed. 'How do you feel?'

'Much too well to be lying down like an invalid,' she admitted stiltedly. 'And I'm starving too.'

'Good.' He paused. 'Does that mean you'll be joining us for dinner?'

'I think so. I still have to meet your mother.' She played with the sash of her dressing gown. 'I—I won't mention Mrs Layton, I give you my word.'

'Thank you.' He was frowning a little. 'I'm sorry to burden you with this, but Vanessa had planned to be away again next week when my mother was due to arrive.'

Cally took a deep breath. 'She's the soul of discretion, isn't she?'

He stared at her. He said slowly, 'You sound as if you blame her for this mess.'

'I'm not out to apportion blame,' Cally told him shortly. 'Besides, it's really none of my business.'

She thought she detected a note of bitterness in his brief sigh, but all he said was, 'Then let's try and have a pleasant meal.' He paused. 'Do you need help to bathe and change?'

She stiffened defensively. 'No—thank you.'

His voice slowed to the drawl she hated. 'Don't get paranoid, darling. I wasn't volunteering. Margaret offered to lend a hand, that's all.'

'That's—kind of her. But I can manage.' Her smile was small and pinched. 'I don't have to be treated with kid gloves. And morning sickness is an inconvenience, not an illness. I'll be fine.'

He got to his feet. 'Then I'll see you downstairs in an hour.'

For a moment Cally thought he was going to bend down and kiss her, and felt the uncontrollable flutter of her pulses. But he simply walked over to the communicating door and disappeared.

Cally stared after him, her lip caught between her teeth. She hadn't simply been lying here on the bed feeling sorry for herself. She'd been working on a strategy designed to detach Nick from her heart and mind, and curb all the stupid, futile longings that still tormented her.

And Dr Hanson's comments about sex had provided her with an emergency plan, which meant that from now on that door was going to become the non-communicating sort, with Nick on one side and herself very firmly on the other.

Because keeping him physically at a distance might be her only means of survival if she was to see the pregnancy deal through to its bitter end.

She would, she thought later, have known Nick's mother anywhere. Dr Tempest was a tall, slender woman, her grey-streaked dark hair drawn severely back from her face into a bun, revealing the elegant chiselling of her face. It was obvious where Nick had got his marvellous bone structure, and those amazing eyes.

Her greeting to her new daughter-in-law, as they met over drinks in the drawing room, was friendly but not overpoweringly so. She was, Cally realised, reserving judgement.

'I think pregnancy was marginally easier in the days when I was having Nick,' she remarked. 'There weren't so many scares and taboos then. But there were no scans either, to tell you the baby's sex. You had to wait for the midwife's pronouncement.' She accepted the martini Nick had mixed for her. 'Do you want to know in advance, Caroline, whether it's a boy or a girl?'

Cally shook her head. 'I—I don't think I mind.'

'Well, I want a girl.' Nick brought her a glass of freshly squeezed orange juice and smiled at her. 'But only if she looks like her mother.'

Cally flushed, and was aware that Dr Tempest's brows had lifted slightly.

Rather overdoing it there, Nick, she told him silently. I'm no one's idea of a beauty. And if, as you claim, this is your one chance, then you'll require a son and heir.

Over dinner, she learned that Dr Tempest would not be spending all her leave with them. She intended to use the Hall as a base, certainly, but her lecture tour would take her all round the British Isles.

She was a wonderful talker, with a droll sense of humour, keeping them endlessly entertained during the meal and the coffee that followed with descriptions of life on the dig, and the various personalities—most of them diametrically opposed to each other—that she had to deal with—and often reconcile.

But Cally was aware at the same time that she was being watched and assessed by that shrewd silvery gaze, and it made her feel uneasy.

She also realised that, however deep in the Guatemalan jungle Dr Tempest had been, she was still *au fait* with what was happening at Wylstone, which meant that she and Nick were in much more regular correspondence than Cally had suspected.

'I hope,' she said at one point, 'that Ranald's abominable widow won't feel obliged to pay a visit while I'm here.'

'Unlikely,' Nick said expressionlessly. 'I gather she's off to the South of France very shortly. I imagine her time up to then will be occupied by shopping and packing.'

Cally looked up, startled. My God, she thought, is there anything he can't manipulate? First Vanessa was due to disappear. Now, more crucially, it's Adele's turn. Because she's the one he needs to keep quiet, and I told him so.

She said steadily, 'Isn't that a rather sudden decision on Adele's part?'

'Not really. She often goes down there.' His mouth curled slightly. 'Regards St Tropez as some kind of spiritual home.'

'Nevertheless,' his mother said drily, 'she's still physically occupying the Dower House, which is unfortunate.'

'Not for much longer, I hope,' Nick said. 'Once I make it

clear I have my own plans for the place.' For a brief moment Cally felt his gaze resting on her.

She swallowed some of the coffee she didn't really want, her mind working furiously. Was that part of his ultimate plan for her? she wondered bleakly. That she should move into the Dower House? Access to the baby strictly on his terms—and while she lived under his supervision? If so, it was an appalling prospect, for all kinds of reasons.

But then, what other options were open to her? Because her original plan—to walk away from the life that had been so summarily imposed on her—was now unthinkable—impossible.

She had realised immediately, even when she'd only suspected that she had conceived, that pregnancy in theory and practice were going to be light years apart. That simply being some kind of surrogate—Nick's temporary breeding machine—was never going to work.

The baby was hers, growing inside her, dependent on her for everything, and giving it up in order to establish a separate life for herself was never going to happen, however bravely she still spoke about the future.

She'd never suspected she could feel like this. That a few weeks could alter her entire way of thinking. She only knew that she could not ever let her baby go—see it brought up by strangers. Especially if one of the strangers turned out to be Vanessa Layton.

Would Nick be cruel enough to do that? she asked herself. Could he? Yet she'd just had proof of how ruthlessly he was prepared to move the pieces round the board in his own private chess game. And soon it would be her turn.

I thought marriage was the trap, she told herself. But I knew nothing. And now I'm caught and helpless.

'You're looking tired, Caroline,' her mother-in-law said quietly. 'Nick, why don't you take your wife up to bed? I think we could all do with an early night.'

'An excellent idea.' Nick held out his hand to Cally, who reluctantly allowed herself to be pulled to her feet. Her heart was thudding awkwardly against her ribcage, protesting over the confrontation that was bound to come.

Unless Nick had read the runes, and decided to stay away of his own accord. But that didn't seem likely.

She said a shy goodnight to Dr Tempest, and was received briefly into a lavender silk embrace spiced with some dry, sophisticated scent she hadn't encountered before.

'It's called *Moi-Meme*,' Nick told her in answer to her halting query, as they went upstairs together. 'And I have to send regular supplies of it to whatever far-flung hellhole Ma finds herself in.' He grinned suddenly. 'She reckons it keeps the snakes at bay. I've sometimes wished I was in advertising. Wouldn't that make the basis of a great campaign?'

Cally had thought she was beyond being amused, yet found herself surprised into laughter. 'Only if there's an outbreak of cobras in Knightsbridge.'

And they arrived at her door in better accord than they'd been for weeks, she thought, with sudden wistfulness. But she couldn't let herself weaken now. It was a case of self-preservation.

She'd expected him to leave her there, and go along to his own quarters, but to her dismay he accompanied her into the lamplit bedroom.

As always, everything was in readiness there, even down to the fresh nightgown laid out across the bed.

Nick picked it up. 'I don't know why Margaret persists with this charade,' he remarked. 'She must know by now that you never wear any of them.'

Cally made herself shrug. 'But then what's one more charade among so many? And she's offering me a choice, which I intend to make in future.' She held out a hand. 'So, may I have it—please?'

He gave her a surprised glance. 'If that's what you want.' His smile was coaxing. Almost tender. 'Don't tell me you're feeling self-conscious,' he added, as he discarded his jacket and began unknotting his tie.

Cally stood beside the bed, clutching the drift of ivory voile against her body.

She took a deep breath. 'What—what are you doing?'

The dark brows lifted. 'Getting undressed. I usually do at bedtime, as you must have noticed by now.'

She touched the tip of her tongue to her lips. 'Didn't Dr Hanson—talk to you?'

'Yes.' Nick was unbuttoning his shirt. 'She suggested a spot of abstinence on my part. Although I suspect it's a little late to worry about that,' he added ruefully. 'However, I won't put the baby in any more jeopardy, I promise.'

'Then why are you here?' She spoke more sharply than she'd planned, and saw him pause, his attention entirely arrested.

He said quietly, 'You're my wife, Cally. This is our bed. Where else should I be?'

'You mean to ignore the doctor?'

'Oh, for God's sake,' he said wearily. 'I was planning a cuddle, not an orgy.'

'And I was counting on a little peace and quiet.' Even to her own ears her voice sounded breathless. 'Now that you—you've achieved your objective, you've no real reason to be here. And I'd hoped my—my privacy might be restored to me.'

He was frighteningly still. He said slowly, 'So—for abstinence, substitute total banishment? Is that it?'

Somehow she lifted her chin. 'Unless you have any objections.'

'So many that it would probably take something like the Domesday Book to list them all,' Nick said icily. 'But I doubt that any of them would do any good, and I'm damned if I'll plead for the right to sleep with you, Cally.'

He picked up his clothing and walked across to the communicating door. 'Would you like me to have a bolt fitted—in case I should forget and stray on to forbidden ground?'

She shook her head, her mouth so dry she felt as if she'd been chewing ashes. 'I'm sure that—won't be necessary.'

His sudden smile seemed to scrape her skin. 'Good guess,'

he said softly. 'And now—goodnight, my little ice angel. Enjoy your dreams—if you can.'

The door closed behind him. Cally sank down on the edge of the bed, staring at the panels, wishing she didn't feel so lost.

It was just the first step, she tried to tell herself. The initial move towards the inevitable, irrevocable separation between them once the baby was born.

Just one of so many difficult decisions ahead of her, she thought achingly.

And the most important of those was to try and find some way, even now, to stop loving him.

CHAPTER TEN

CALLY gave her pillows a last ineffectual punch, then sat bolt upright, glaring into the darkness. She said aloud, 'Oh, this is ridiculous.'

She was tired to the bone, so why, then, couldn't she sleep? At one moment she'd felt too hot, so she'd kicked off the covers. The next she was dragging them back because she was cold, which was ludicrous on a warm summer night.

She'd turned so restlessly and so constantly from one side to the other that her nightgown had become twisted around her, imprisoning her like a straitjacket, and the damned pillows felt as if they were filled with lead instead of feathers.

She'd closed her eyes so tightly that they ached, but it was useless. She was still wide awake, and she knew why.

Because with Nick gone, the big bed seemed a vast empty wasteland. Subconsciously, she realised, she was reaching for him, and finding only loneliness. And it was no good telling herself that it was something she had to get accustomed to, when she might as well be lying on razorblades.

I can't go on like this, she told herself, wriggling to the edge of the tumbled bed. She freed herself with difficulty from the stranglehold of her nightdress, shaking out its folds, then reached into the drawer of the night table for the torch that was kept there in case of power cuts. After all, she didn't want to attract too much attention by putting on main lights, she thought as she trod silently across the room to the communicating door.

She paused in the passageway, listening, but there was no sound from the room at the far end, and it seemed safe to slip into the bathroom.

She hadn't investigated all the mirrored cupboards too minutely, but she knew one of them held first aid materials, so surely there had to be some kind of medication that might help her. Somehow she had to get some rest, she told herself through gritted teeth as she switched on the torch and began her search. But, apart from some basic painkillers, there was nothing. Not even a cold remedy.

Nick, it seemed, didn't suffer from the ordinary human ailments—and certainly not insomnia.

Cursing under her breath, she pushed the tubes of antiseptic and packets of plasters to one side, so that she could reach the back of the glass shelf, only to find them spilling out on to the tiled surface beneath, knocking over various jars and bottles on their way and sending Nick's aftershave crashing into the basin.

In the stillness of the night, the noise seemed like a thunderclap, Cally thought frantically. She made a grab to stop other containers rolling on to the floor and dropped the torch, which promptly went out.

'Oh, no,' she wailed under her breath, as she went down on her knees, feeling for it in the darkness.

Only to find, almost before she could draw another breath, the bathroom flooded with sudden light and Nick's astonished voice saying, 'What the hell...?'

She looked round defensively as she retrieved the torch. 'I'm sorry. I was trying to be quiet.'

'Heaven forbid you ever try to be noisy.' His tone was caustic. He walked forward, tightening the sash of his robe, and inspected the broken bottle of aftershave in the basin. 'Pretty drastic measures,' he commented. 'I didn't realise you disliked it so much. I can't say I care for it much at this strength.'

'It was an accident,' she muttered, scrambling to her feet. 'I was just looking for something to help me sleep.'

'Were you indeed?' Nick said, too pleasantly. 'I'm afraid you won't find it, and even if you did you're taking nothing that hasn't been prescribed for you, because I won't let you. Do I make myself clear?' He waited while she nodded reluctantly. 'Now, go back to bed,' he directed, 'while I clean up this mess.' He walked past her and opened the bathroom window.

'What's the point of going to bed when I can't sleep?' Cally said rebelliously.

Nick looked at her, sighing faintly. 'Maybe you should keep off coffee after dinner,' he said. 'Would hot milk help? Shall I fetch some for you?'

'I—I don't know.' She hesitated. 'I've already caused you enough trouble.'

He said curtly, 'You don't know the half of it.' He came over to her, and before she could stop him picked her up in his arms and started back with her to her room.

'My God,' he said, halting as he surveyed the rumpled bed. 'It looks like a disaster area.' He put her into a chair and began straightening the sheets with brisk efficiency. She watched him as he plumped the pillows and folded back the tangled cover into inviting neatness.

Treating her like a child, she thought, when she needed so desperately to be a woman. His woman.

'There you are, Lady Tempest.' He glanced at her with faint mockery when he'd finished. 'Your chaste couch awaits you. Now I'll get your milk.'

When he'd gone, she got into bed, sitting back against the banked up pillows, arranging the sheet carefully, so that most of her was covered. Not that he seemed to care that she was wearing nothing but a transparent layer of voile, she thought. He'd hardly even looked at her. But probably that was just as well, considering the doctor's advice.

But earlier he'd wanted to sleep with her—nothing more. And she knew now, with total certainty, that she wanted it too—so badly. Longed to feel his arms around her, holding her close and safely.

Vanessa Layton was a beautiful woman, but she, Cally, had her own weapons. She was Nick's wife, for God's sake, and carrying his child. And that had to matter,

So why had she conceded victory so readily to her rival? She loved Nick desperately, so why wasn't she prepared to fight for him? To try and make a marriage out of the shambles of their lives?

And persuading Nick back into her bed seemed an obvious beginning, she thought, slipping off her nightgown and tossing it to the floor, where he'd be bound to see it when he returned. And if that wasn't enough—well, surely she'd learned enough from their nights together to tempt him back to her.

He returned quite soon, carrying a porcelain beaker which he handed to her. 'Hot milk,' he said, 'with honey and a pinch of cinnamon and nutmeg. Just like Nanny used to make.' Then he bent and picked up her nightdress, placing it on the bed.

Concealing her chagrin, Cally accepted the beaker with a murmur of thanks. 'You had a nanny?'

'I had loads of them,' he said. 'On the whole, I preferred the older plainer ones. They tended to be around for longer,' he added, his mouth twisting cynically.

She sipped her milk, which was as delicious as it was comforting. 'Your mother didn't bring you up?'

'Ma started pursuing her career again while I was still quite young,' he said. 'As I got older I realised why. Marriage to my father was tricky at best. Most of the time it must have been impossible.' He shrugged. 'I'm sorry. Bedtime stories are supposed to have a happy ending.' He gave her a brief smile. 'I hope the milk does the trick. Goodnight, Cally.'

'Nick.' She put the empty beaker down on the night table and clutched at the sleeve of his robe as he turned away. 'Nick—don't leave me, please.' The sheet fell away, baring her breasts. Kiss me, she pleaded silently, touch me.

The dark face was suddenly expressionless. 'A few hours ago you couldn't wait to be rid of me.'

She tried to smile. 'I—I was feeling a little wobbly. Put it down to the hormones.'

'Or perhaps the same instinct that made you run away from me last year.' The grey eyes watched her steadily. 'Maybe you were right all along, Cally. Your grandfather would certainly have thought so.'

'Grandfather?' she echoed. 'What do you mean?'

He moved to the chair she'd vacated and sat down. 'I went to him,' he said quietly. 'Told him I wanted to marry you and asked his permission to court you—pay my addresses—some suitably old-fashioned phrase. I thought he'd appreciate that. But I was wrong. He made it very clear in a few well-chosen words of his own that I wasn't fit to come near you, and that he'd do his damnedest to ensure that I never did.'

'He said that?' The breath caught in her throat. 'But why?'

'Oh, he had a whole list of reasons.' Nick examined a fleck on his nail. 'He was quite embarrassingly frank. I was too old for you, and altogether too shop-soiled, he said. He condemned my past, discounted my future, and had some harsh words about my present lifestyle. He wanted, he said, a decent lad for his precious girl. And when I suggested, quite mildly, that two virgins together wasn't always a recipe for happiness, he called me a foul-minded bastard and ordered me out of the house.'

He paused. 'It seems there'd also been a problem with my father. Years ago, he unwisely attempted to try it on with your mother. It got him nowhere, but it was an incident that clearly still rankled and it tarred me with the same brush.'

He sent her a faint smile. 'But believe that you were precious to him, Cally, even if he didn't always show it. I think he was simply trying to protect you. And, on balance, he was probably right.'

She said huskily, 'When was this?'

'Not very far into our acquaintance. Just before you decided to go and live in London, as it happens. I thought perhaps your grandfather had told you he'd warned me off, and you were taking yourself out of harm's way.'

'You just—faded out of my life,' she said slowly. 'There was a dance, and you never came near me all evening. I didn't even see you out riding.'

'You were out of bounds,' Nick said. 'And I wanted to prove to your grandfather, and myself, that I was still capable of behaving decently.'

He shook his head. 'Then your grandfather got sick, and all your other problems started piling up. I should have stuck to my guns and stayed away. Instead I decided I could—help. I've thought since it must have maddened your grandfather to discover he was in any way beholden to me, and I'm sorry for that. And as a result here we are today, in this unholy bloody mess.'

He gave a swift, harsh laugh. 'It's all my own fault, of course. I should have accepted your belated change of heart and let you go. Given you a quick, quiet divorce. Not dragged you back here and inflicted this latest disaster on you.'

He got to his feet. 'I wonder if your grandfather would have approved of Kit Matlock—thought he was decent enough for you.'

'Kit?' she repeated incredulously. 'But I never considered him like that. Not once, I swear it.'

'Well, it's not important now. We have to think about this baby I've forced on you.' He stared down at the floor. 'It may not be an appropriate time for this, but maybe your lack of sleep is caused by worry—about the future. And I want you to know that there's no need. Not any more. All the things I said once about custody—well, let's say I was angry. Because I would never take the baby away from you, Cally, not unless that was what you wished. If you decided to opt for a different kind of life, without the burden of an unwanted child.'

She gasped. 'I would never do that.'

The situation was slipping away from her. No, she thought, not slipping—galloping down to some kind of destruction. She could feel it.

She said pleadingly, 'Nick—listen…'

He held up a silencing hand. 'Let me finish—please. You can live wherever you wish—have whatever money you require. It will all be taken care of. I hope that you'll allow me regular visits, establish in our baby's mind that he or she has a father. Perhaps we can even create some kind of working relationship between us.'

He moved towards the door. 'And now that your mind's at rest, maybe you'll be able to sleep.'

Cally said his name again, but she spoke to an empty room.

A microcosm of the empty life which was suddenly yawning in front of her, she thought with despair. And she was frightened.

'Well, I think that's a good morning's work,' Cecily Tempest said with satisfaction. 'Lunch is now indicated. Why don't you grab us a table at the Unicorn while I take all these parcels back to the car? You can order for me, Cally—some of their home-baked ham with salad. It's too hot for anything else. Oh, and a spritzer,' she threw over her shoulder as she moved off in the direction of the car park.

Smiling, Cally lifted a hand in acknowledgement and turned in the opposite direction, making her way towards the High Street and its sixteenth-century inn.

It was the first real shopping spree she'd indulged in since she'd bought her trousseau. She still hadn't worn half the clothes she'd bought then and probably she never would, because nothing fitted her any more.

There was a boutique near the cathedral called Great Expectations, and under her mother-in-law's approving eye she'd picked out some well-cut trousers and tops, and a few pretty dresses to see her through the middle of her pregnancy. At the very end, when the weather was cold, she'd simply get some large sweaters, she thought, and use them as camouflage.

If things had been different she might even have borrowed from Nick...

She bit her lip. She was trespassing on forbidden ground here. She and Nick were polite strangers who sometimes shared a roof, and she had to accept that—come to terms with it—because there was no alternative.

'A working relationship', he'd said. She presumed that was what he'd been trying to establish over these past weeks, because while he treated her with friendliness and consideration there was certainly no intimacy between them. The risk zone was well behind them now, but Nick never came to her room, even though she'd started leaving the communicating door open as tacit encouragement. She'd been tempted, often and often, to go to him instead, but the very real fear of rejection prevented her.

But if her emotional life seemed to have reached its nadir, her pregnancy was going well now. Her sickness had suddenly stopped, but she was still sleeping badly, alone in that huge bed, and Dr Hanson, concerned, had prescribed the mildest of sedatives on a strictly temporary basis in order to break the pattern of insomnia.

But the drug that would cure the heartache and loneliness which were Cally's real problem had yet to be invented.

Not that Nick was at the Hall a great deal these days, she thought. He'd seemingly thrown himself completely back into his work, and was involved in a lot of business trips. Getting her used to life without him, she supposed.

Cecily Tempest came and went as her lecture tour permitted. The fund-raising had gone well, and she would soon be returning to Guatemala, although she'd promised to return for the baby's birth.

And to say goodbye, if she did but know it, Cally thought drearily as she turned into the High Street. After an initial sticky period she had managed to create a rapport with Nick's mother, whom she'd been told to call by her first name, and found herself genuinely enjoying her company. She would miss her, she told herself, even if it was only for a few months.

Halfway along the street there was a Victorian shopping arcade with a high stained glass roof, and Cally was glad to escape into its shade for a few minutes to look in the window of a babywear shop that had recently opened.

She had opted not to know the sex of the baby in advance, but as she looked at the heart-wrenching display of small garments in traditional blues and pinks, she found herself wondering if she'd made the right decision. She'd asked Nick's opinion, but he'd politely deferred to her, which was no help at all.

I could always change my mind, she thought, admiring an exquisite lace christening robe.

With a sigh, she turned towards the heat and glare of the

High Street, and halted, eyes narrowing in shock behind her glasses. On the far side of the street there was a short row of Georgian houses, now transformed into offices, and Nick had just emerged from one of them, his arm round the shoulders of Vanessa Layton, who was walking beside him.

As she watched, Cally saw him bend his head slightly and drop a light kiss on his companion's hair. She smiled back at him and put up a hand to touch his cheek. Then they parted, walking away in opposite directions.

Everything about the little scene was deeply and irrevocably etched into Cally's mind. The body language said it all, she thought. She was permitted no physical contact with her husband, but Vanessa could stand close to him, stroke his face, and smile into his eyes—all gestures that epitomised a close and familiar intimacy, that had nothing to do with mere lust.

He loves her, she thought. He really loves her, and I've never had a prayer. For him, my only plus mark is that I've turned out to be fertile.

She found suddenly that she was fighting for breath. Nick wasn't even supposed to be in Clayminster today, she thought wildly. He was scheduled to visit Wellingford, checking on the progress of Gunners Wharf.

In fact, she'd asked if she might go with him, but he'd responded briefly that it would be pointless as he only intended a flying visit.

'Want to send anyone your love?' he'd asked with faint mockery as he rose from the breakfast table.

Cally had lifted her chin. 'Yes,' she'd responded coolly. 'Tracy, if you happen to see her.'

Had Vanessa gone with him? she wondered. Was that why she herself had been turned down? Or had the planned visit been subordinated to some alternative scheme of his lover's making?

She came slowly out of the arcade and leaned for a moment on the corner of the window, struggling to regain her equilibrium. After all, she derided herself, what had the last few moments told her that she didn't already know?

I could just do with not having my nose rubbed in it quite so publicly, she thought, swallowing.

'Caroline? Cally, my dear, are you all right?' Cecily Tempest appeared beside her, her face concerned.

Cally was aware of an almost overwhelming urge to bury her head on her mother-in-law's shoulder and sob out her hurt and heartbreak. But that, of course, was impossible. She'd given her word to keep silent on the situation, and she couldn't break it, whatever emotional damage she might be suffering.

She gave Cecily a wavering smile. 'You were quite right about the heat. It's sweltering.'

'Then let's forget about lunch here and go home,' the older woman said decisively. 'Margaret will be able to rustle up a salad for us.'

Cally was glad to find herself in the car, being quietly driven back to Wylstone through the lanes. She leaned back, closing her eyes, trying to erase today's least welcome image from her memory.

'So,' Cecily Tempest said at last, 'would this be a good time to tell me what's really the matter? Because something undoubtedly is.'

Startled, Cally sat up and prepared for defence. 'I don't know what you mean.'

Cecily sighed. 'Cally, please don't take me for a fool. You're young, you're in love, and having your first baby. Life should be perfect. Instead, you're so determinedly bright that you almost dazzle me into thinking you're happy. And Nick, on the few occasions that he lowers his guard these days, looks as if he's living through some personal nightmare.'

'Perhaps—perhaps he's having business worries.'

'Nonsense,' his mother said tartly. 'His companies are making an obscene amount of money. If he never worked another day he'd still be a wealthy man. So why is he pushing himself, as he undoubtedly is, when he could be relaxing for a while and enjoying this unique time with you?'

Cally shrugged. 'I don't know. We haven't really discussed it...'

'Or much else, from what I can see.' There was another silence, then Dr Tempest said, more gently, 'Cally, I'm aware that you spent your first year of marriage apart. I realise I'm not supposed to know, but Nick's godfather, a very dear friend, got to hear of it, and wrote me a concerned letter. My son's own correspondence made no reference to the fact that he was living alone, so when I discovered that you were now together again I decided not to pursue the point. To let sleeping dogs lie.

'And I would still,' she went on candidly, 'except that the dogs appear to have woken up, and are circling each other, gearing up for a fight. I don't want to be forced to send for a bucket of cold water.'

'Nick would never fight with me.' Cally permitted herself a reluctant smile. 'He's far too civilised.'

'Don't count on it,' Dr Tempest advised. 'One day he might surprise you. Or you might surprise him,' she added thoughtfully. 'If the façade ever snaps.'

She became brisk again. 'But I won't press you any further, dear girl. I just can't believe Nick isn't taking steps to remedy the situation. He was appalled when he realised what was happening in my marriage to his father, and swore to me that he would never marry unless he could make his wife so happy that she'd never know an anxious moment.'

She added drily, 'He seems to have fallen well short of that ideal, but I'm damned if I can see why.'

Cally turned away to look out of the window. Oh, God, she thought, if you knew—if you only knew… But at least you still have your illusions about him, whereas I—I have none.

When they arrived back at the Hall, Cally said mendaciously that she wasn't hungry and went up to the bedroom, supposedly to rest. But she was unable to settle. Her thoughts were far too busy—and too wretched.

Instead, she decided to take a shower, then change into the coolest of the new dresses she'd acquired that morning. It was made from a thin cotton material, in an attractive pale turquoise colour, and the style was button-through, with a discreetly high waist.

Designed to conceal a multitude of sins, Cally thought, viewing herself in the mirror.

She'd go downstairs, she thought next, and try to convince her mother-in-law that the marriage was just experiencing a few teething troubles which would soon be resolved. It was what she wanted to hear, and she just might believe it.

But the house seemed deserted, although the remains of lunch were still laid out in the dining room. Cally helped herself to a plate of cold chicken and potato salad, and took it out on to the terrace, seating herself at a table with a sun umbrella. The baby, she told herself, would not appreciate her skipping meals, whatever the reason.

She was just finishing a dish of strawberries when she realised with a sinking heart that she wasn't alone any more, and that Adele was sauntering across the lawn towards her. She was wearing a smart figure-hugging dress in *café au lait* linen, and carried a broad-brimmed straw hat, which she was using to fan herself.

'Hi, there.' Her tone was casual, but her eyes were sharp as they flicked over the younger woman. 'All alone? No happy little family gathering today?'

'As you see,' Cally said shortly.

'I see that you're putting on weight, certainly. Heavens, Cally, you're going to be the size of a house if you don't watch it.'

'My weight gain,' Cally said levelly, 'is absolutely normal.'

Adele shrugged. 'If you say so. But it's hardly any wonder that Nick prefers to spend his time elsewhere these days.' She paused. 'I suppose he's told you that I'm going?'

'No,' Cally said slowly, still smarting from the previous jibe. 'He hasn't mentioned it.'

'Then you heard it from me first.' Adele sat down on the chair opposite. 'I'm moving down to an apartment near St Tropez, my dear. Far more my style than that dreary Dower

House, and more than I can actually afford, but Nick's stirred himself to be generous for once. *Et voilà*.'

She smiled. 'I gather he needs the Dower House vacated for some purpose of his own. I thought you might know what it was.'

'Why should I?' Cally found the last of the strawberries over-sweet, and pushed her plate away.

'Well, it's always been the place where the Tempests dump their unwanted women—once they've served their purpose.' Adele yawned. 'I'd say you'd make the ideal candidate, once you've produced the heir and Nick pensions you off.' Her eyes, bright with malice, met Cally's. 'That is what he's planning—isn't it?'

'I wouldn't know,' Cally said quietly. 'I don't have your genius for intelligence-gathering.'

'Oh, it won't happen quite yet, naturally,' Adele went on languidly. 'The place isn't ready for immediate occupation, particularly as I'm sure your taste in décor and mine are poles apart. But I guess Nick will be putting in his personal design consultant for the makeover.' Her smile was sly. 'I wonder what colour she'll pick for the nursery? Green, I dare say. You must drop me a postcard and let me know.'

She got to her feet. 'Well, I have things to do before I leave in the morning, so perhaps you'll make my farewells for me.'

'Of course,' Cally said, her voice wooden. 'Goodbye.'

'*Adieu* to you too.' Adele lingered for a moment. 'You know, I feel quite sorry for you, Cally. You've been dealt a rotten hand, and no one's told you the rules of the game, but you're still putting up your own pathetic fight. It's almost—admirable. So, good luck with the Dower House. I think you'll need it.'

Cally sat motionless, watching her walk away across the lawn, her figure dwindling into the distance. When she was sure the other woman was out of sight, and out of earshot, she rose slowly and stiffly from her chair and went back into the drawing room.

She stood for a moment, looking round, until her eye fell on a large Worcester bowl reposing on a small table.

She picked it up by the rim. She said aloud, quietly and conversationally, 'I think I've had enough.'

Then she drew back her arm and sent the bowl flying towards the fireplace.

CHAPTER ELEVEN

HER aim, for once, was unerring. The bowl hit the heavy stone mantelshelf and shattered, sending a hundred noisy fragments cascading on to the hearth.

She stood, panting a little, regarding the havoc she'd created. Aware at the same time that there were footsteps in the hall, approaching fast. The drawing room door was flung wide as Nick strode in. He'd clearly been back for some time, because the dark business suit he'd been wearing earlier had been replaced by jeans and a casual shirt.

'What the hell...?' he began furiously, then checked, his narrowed gaze scanning his wife, who was standing with her hands clenched and her eyes blazing out of her pale face, then moving to the debris on the hearth.

'Another accident?' he asked.

'No,' she said, the word swift and staccato. 'And what are you doing here?'

'I live here,' he said. 'Or I have what passes for a life.'

'But you were supposed to be going to Wellingford.'

He shrugged. 'Something happened that I needed to attend to. I'll go tomorrow.' He looked back at the hearth. 'So how did it happen?'

'I did it on purpose.' Cally lifted her chin stormily. 'Because I felt like it,' she added for good measure.

'Really?' Nick's brows lifted. 'And did you find it therapeutic? Maybe I should try it.' He walked to the fireplace and took a porcelain figurine from the mantelshelf. 'I've never liked this,' he said, almost conversationally. He took a couple of long strides backwards, then shied it. It broke with a satisfying crack, and the small head rolled sadly across the hearth.

Cally found she was holding her breath as she watched.

'No,' he said, after a second's pause. 'Sadly, that doesn't do it for me. But don't let me stop you wrecking the place in your quest for fulfilment,' he added, too pleasantly. 'In the meantime, perhaps I can find mine in other ways.'

The next moment Cally found herself scooped up into his arms and dumped down on to the yielding softness of one of the sofas, while he stood over her and made to unfasten the belt of his jeans with stark and unmistakable purpose in his dark face.

Something froze inside her. 'Oh, God.' She struggled upright. 'Are you mad? Don't—don't you dare touch me!'

'Why not?' His tone bit. 'What have I got to lose?'

She didn't look at him. She said with difficulty. 'Maybe— the woman you're supposed to love.'

'The woman I do love.' The bitterness in his voice made her flinch. 'The woman I shall love to the end of my life, God help me.'

The pain of that made her voice falter. 'And, besides, you— we—might hurt the baby.'

'Ah, yes,' he said harshly. 'Our child.' He turned and moved away to the sofa opposite. Sat down. 'However, I think any lasting damage might well be to each other.'

There was a pause, then he said, 'I was actually coming to find you when I heard the crash. It seems to me there are matters we need to discuss.'

'Let me guess,' Cally said. 'Could one of them be the Dower House?'

His brows lifted. 'Well—yes. But how did you know?'

'I've had a visit from Adele,' she said. 'She came to tell me she was leaving. She even made it sound as if you'd paid her off.'

'Really?' He sounded politely interested. 'Then for once she was actually telling the truth.'

Cally gasped. 'You mean you—bribed her into going?'

'I bought her an apartment in the South of France and agreed to pay her removal expenses on condition that she takes that old witch of a housekeeper with her and that neither of them return.'

She said faintly, 'My God.'

'You disapprove?' He shrugged a shoulder. 'Now, I felt it was money well spent.'

'Of course,' she said. 'Especially as it frees up the Dower House.' She threw back her head. 'You don't have much mercy, do you, Nick? Can't you imagine what it will be like for me—what it will do to me—living so near—seeing you all the time? Seeing you with *her*.' The word seemed to explode out of her as her voice rose. 'Is she going to be moving into the Hall with you—part of the ''working relationship'' you mentioned? Is that the cosy plan?'

She shook her head. 'Just—don't ask her to do any interior design work for the Dower House, that's all. In fact, don't let her take one step over the threshold. Because I really couldn't stand that—not again. This time I'm choosing my own colours, my own décor. And your mistress will not—*not*—be involved.'

Out of the corner of her eye she was aware of movement— a shadow falling across the carpet.

She looked round and to her horror saw Cecily Tempest standing at the French windows. Saw her face frozen in shock, and realised she must have heard everything as she crossed the terrace.

'My mistress? Cally—what the hell are you talking about?' Nick said hoarsely.

'Oh, I forgot,' she flung back at him. 'I wasn't supposed to let the cat out of the bag, of course.' She got unsteadily to her feet. 'I'm sorry, Cecily. I apologise for breaking the taboo. For mentioning her in your presence. For once speaking the terrible, unsayable truth.'

She took a choking breath. 'But you see I can't go on pretending. Not any more. I can't go on letting people think that everything's all right when I'm dying—bloody *dying* inside.'

'Cally, my poor girl.' Her mother-in-law's voice was warmly compassionate. 'You're surely not talking about Vanessa Layton?'

Cally squared her shoulders. 'Yes, but I truly didn't mean you to hear,' she said quietly. 'I—I suppose I forgot that Nick and I weren't alone in the house. I—I'm so sorry.'

Dr Tempest turned to her son. 'Nick—what on earth is this?'

He spread his hands almost helplessly. 'I swear I haven't the faintest idea. She—Cally—can't have thought such a thing.'

Cally rounded on him. 'How can you say that?' she demanded, her voice hoarse. 'When I saw you with her—on our wedding day. Adele told me where you were—what you were doing—so I went there—I went to the cottage. I saw you holding her in your arms—heard what you were saying—what you promised. Everything.' She swallowed convulsively. 'Then you took her up to the bedroom and I watched you at the window—drawing the curtains so that you could be with her just hours after you married me. And that—that's when I ran away.'

There was a silence, then Nick said, 'Oh, dear God,' as horrified comprehension dawned in his face. 'Adele told you *that*?'

'The Dowager Lady Tempest seems to have a great deal to answer for,' Cecily Tempest said grimly. 'But at least, my dear Nick, you have dealt with that particular problem. After tomorrow she'll be out of your lives, and incapable of doing any more harm. As for this beloved girl of yours,' she went on. 'The time has come for total honesty, I think, and I feel very strongly that the truth should come from me.'

She walked across to Cally and took her cold hands in hers, urging her to sit down again. 'My dear child, Vanessa Layton is not and never could be Nick's mistress. But a relationship does exist which Nick, out of consideration for my feelings, has always tried to keep hidden from me.'

She took a deep breath. 'You see, Cally, Vanessa is Nick's half-sister. My late husband's illegitimate child by the woman who was once his secretary.'

Cally stared at her. 'His—sister?' Her voice was barely a whisper.

Nick said roughly, 'Cally—I tried to tell you, but you refused to discuss it. You said you already knew about it—from Adele.' He banged his clenched fist into the palm of his other hand. 'I should have realised that if that arch-bitch had really known the truth she'd have seen it as a golden opportunity for blackmail.' He looked at his mother. 'But you—you knew? And said nothing to me all this time?'

'Yes,' Dr Tempest said firmly. 'I've always known about Vanessa. But my ridiculous pride would never let me admit it before. I was even content to let you go on sheltering me in my supposed ignorance. But in the light of all this sadness— these terrible misunderstandings—all that no longer matters. It's time we all stopped pretending.'

Nick's tone was strained. 'Mother, I—I can't believe this. How did you find out?'

'In the usual sordid way,' his mother said ruefully. 'I used a private detective. Oh, I was accustomed to your father's endless philandering—all the one-night stands that he assured me weren't important to him, even though they mattered to me, hurt me very deeply.'

She shook her head. 'But somehow I knew instinctively that the relationship with Barbara Miller was different. And I told myself that I deserved to discover the truth.' Her smile was sad. 'Perhaps I even believed it. I certainly wasn't expecting details of a full-blown liaison that had been going on for months, ever since her husband had gone abroad on some academic exchange scheme. Because, frankly, that wasn't how it worked with Graham. It was invariably a brief fling, then back to me to play the repentant model husband. But not this time. He was moody, preoccupied. Too distracted to cover his tracks properly.

'The report from the detective explained why. Apparently, Barbara was pregnant, and Graham, who had totally refused to have more children after Nick was born, was jubilant. Planning, in fact, a whole new life with this younger woman.'

Cally's heart was resounding like a triphammer, and she couldn't look at Nick. She didn't dare in case the tight knot of misery in her chest exploded in tears.

She said shakily, 'Cecily—please. Don't do this to yourself. There's no need…'

'Ah, but there is,' her mother-in-law corrected quite gently. 'It's something I should have spoken about a long time ago, instead of burdening my poor Nick with all this guilty secrecy—and nearly wrecking his life into the bargain.'

She looked down at her hands, twisting the thin platinum wedding ring. 'At the time, my dears, that was the very last straw—the moment when I decided to accept that my marriage was over and resume my own life, my career.'

Nick went on staring at her. 'But there was no divorce.'

'He never asked me,' Cecily said simply. 'Because Mrs Miller changed her mind and decided to stay with her own husband.' Her mouth curled slightly. 'Apparently she'd been to the States to visit him, and would therefore be able to convince him the baby was his. Very convenient. Later, I gather, she came to regret her decision, and the affair was resumed. Graham even secretly contributed to his daughter's support,' she added with a faint grimace. 'But there was no more talk of marriage, and by this time I was spending the greater part of my time abroad, and wasn't around to be caused more pain.

'But I still couldn't let it go somehow. Then Barbara died, and her husband moved away, so your father was forced to lose touch with Vanessa. And I presumed—hoped—that would be the end of it. That I would never again have to acknowledge the existence of this child who wasn't mine. I hadn't allowed, of course, for Graham confiding in Nick—making him become involved too.' She smiled at her son. 'Wasn't that what happened?'

Nick nodded, his face sombre. 'It was when Dad was dying. He sent for me—made me promise that I'd find her—be a brother to her. Make sure she wanted for nothing. But all in the strictest confidence. Neither you nor Geoffrey Miller were ever to find out.' His laugh was brief and harsh. 'I wasn't happy about it, but in the end I did as he wanted. And I really thought I'd managed it, until now.'

'I was very angry with you at first,' his mother said. 'But I soon came to see that you were trying to behave decently in an impossible situation. More sinned against than sinning. Also that it had all happened a long time ago, and really didn't matter any more.'

She sighed. 'I only wish I'd told you so, there and then, and saved all this heartache. We could easily have left that nice, trusting man Geoffrey Miller in his fool's paradise. I quite saw that he shouldn't be wounded in such an appalling way. But I—I should have had the guts to be honest.'

She was silent for a moment, then she shook herself, as if she was dispensing with unpleasant memories.

'And now, my darlings, you have to be honest with each other.' Her tone was brisk. 'Nick dear, I suggest you take your wife somewhere quiet and private, and try to set the record straight.' She reached for the newspaper lying beside her on the sofa and folded it at the crossword. 'I'll tell Margaret not to wait dinner for you,' she added serenely.

Cally's breathing seemed to stop suddenly. She felt angry, remorseful and scared, all at the same time. So she'd been wrong—completely and terribly wrong—about Vanessa Layton, but that changed nothing else. There was still a huge unhappy question mark hanging over her marriage. And being alone with Nick—as past experience had shown—was no guarantee she would receive the answers her lonely, frightened heart demanded.

Was it the kind of risk she could really afford? But was there any way out?

'Cally?' Nick was standing in front of her, his expression unfathomable, his hand held out in inflexible demand.

Without a scene in front of Cecily, who'd surely suffered enough traumas for one day, there was little she could do. So, with what dignity she could command, she allowed herself to be helped to her feet and led from the room.

In the hall, she said breathlessly, 'Shall we—talk in your study?'

'It's not very private, and rarely quiet,' he said. 'I have a better idea.'

As they reached the stairs she tried to pull away. 'Nick—

this is silly. It's the middle of the afternoon. People don't go to their bedrooms at this time of day.'

'Yes, they do,' he said. 'If they want to make love.'

'But I don't.' It emerged almost as a bleat, she realised bitterly.

'Tough,' Nick said pleasantly. 'Then you'll just have to lie still and think about something else, won't you, darling? Why not give circumstantial evidence some consideration?'

Cally bit her lip, giving him a mutinous glare. 'Everything's a joke to you. But I had good reason to think as I did. Today you said you'd be in Wellingford, yet I saw you with her— with Vanessa in Clayminster High Street. I saw how you behaved towards each other. It—it looked like love.'

'It's a kind of love,' he said quietly, after a pause. 'We share the same blood, and we've been through hell together. That— engenders affection.'

He closed the bedroom door behind them. 'Tell me something, Cally. Why blindly accept the word of a woman who's never liked you, yet condemn me out of hand? Why didn't you just march up the path a year ago, hammer on the door, and demand to know what was going on?'

She walked over to the dressing table, rearranging brushes and combs with nervous fingers. She sent him a sideways glance. 'Would you have told me?'

'Yes, of course,' he said instantly. 'Although it would have been unfair, in some ways, to burden you with such a secret so soon in the marriage. The original plan was that Vanessa should come to the wedding and that we'd explain the whole thing to you together. When she didn't turn up as promised, I called her mobile. She was at the clinic, and in a terrible state. They'd sent for her, only to tell her that there was a less than one per cent chance of Tony ever regaining consciousness, and that if he did he'd be seriously brain damaged. It was the first time they'd suggested doing away with life-support.

'She'd been living on hope, waiting for a miracle, and suddenly it was all snatched away from her.' He walked over to the window and stood staring down into the gardens below.

Both of them, Cally realised, were staying well away from the bed.

'I don't think it even registered that it was our wedding day—not then, anyway,' Nick went on. 'She begged me to come and collect her, because she was in no fit state to drive home. It was the first time she'd really needed me, and I told myself I couldn't let her down. That I'd be there and back before you knew it, and that anyway we had the rest of our lives to look forward to, when she had nothing. I convinced myself that you'd understand. That I might even earn myself some brownie points when I explained.

'So, I called her doctor and requested him to meet us at the cottage. I also arranged for her car to be picked up and returned. When she'd seen the doctor I drove over to the pharmacy and brought back the sedatives he'd prescribed. I managed to persuade her to take one, and then go upstairs to lie down.'

He gave her an ironic look. 'The point, I guess, at which you arrived and drew your own conclusions. I don't blame you for that, Cally. But you should have confronted me—given me the chance to explain. Not just run away without a word.'

She didn't look at him. 'Didn't Adele tell you she'd sent me to the cottage?'

'Adele wasn't at the Hall when I returned,' Nick said. 'I'd made it clear that I didn't want either her, or the other resident witch, anywhere near the place for twenty-four hours, until we'd left on our honeymoon. She was supposed to be gone when we got back from the church. I simply thought she'd done as she was told.'

He paused. 'It's time for the truth, Cally,' he said slowly. 'Why did you—just leave? Were you really convinced you couldn't live with me—and was seeing me with poor Vanessa simply the excuse you needed? I—I have to know.'

Her voice was unsteady. 'I need to know something, too, Nick. Why did you marry me? Was I just the first available girl—someone who'd be grateful to be favoured by the glamorous Nick Tempest and who wouldn't interfere in your life too much?'

He turned to look at her, the skin taut over his cheekbones, anguish in his grey gaze.

He said, 'Cally, I fell in love with you the moment I saw you glaring down at me from the back of your horse that first day. I was severely tempted to drag you out of the saddle and ravish you in the bracken there and then. Instead I behaved incredibly well, and tried to ask for your grandfather's permission. I told you that.'

'Yes—but you never told me you loved me.' She spread her hands almost helplessly. 'Not even once. You never—mentioned the word.'

He sighed. 'My lovely one, how could I? Bad things were happening to you, one after the other, and making passionate advances to you seemed totally inappropriate—particularly when you were mourning your grandfather.'

His mouth twisted. 'I decided to wait until we had moonlight, and a beach, and maybe palm trees. And then I'd go on my knees and tell you exactly how much I loved you. Lay my heart at your feet.'

He paused again. 'Besides,' he said carefully, 'I thought I'd made my intentions—and my feelings—quite clear when we went on that picnic. That was the third part of my plan.'

'You had a plan?' She shook her head. 'I don't understand.'

'My sweet,' Nick said gently. 'You were so young, you almost broke my heart. So I told myself I had to take it easy. First—I had to get you to like me. Second—I needed you to trust me. I thought—I hoped—that I'd succeeded pretty well in both of them. Then, thirdly, of course, I wanted you to enjoy being in bed with me.' He grimaced. 'I told myself afterwards I should have made that my first priority. That everything else would have naturally followed.

'But you didn't hesitate to face me down that first day, Cally. So why the hell didn't you confront me over Vanessa?' His voice was suddenly husky. 'I can only think it was because you didn't care enough, and if that's true, I don't know how

I'm going to bear it. How I'm going to be able to live the rest of my life without you.'

She said softly, 'I didn't dare ask. I was too afraid of what your answer might be to take the risk. I just wanted to get away as far as possible and die, because you'd broken my heart. You see, I fell in love with you, too, Nick—that first day.' A smile trembled on her lips. 'And I'm sorry you decided against the bracken.'

For the first time his own mouth relaxed into the ghost of his old grin. 'On reflection, it was the right choice. Bloody uncomfortable, bracken. Sheets are infinitely preferable, and pillows—and you, my love,' he added softly. 'My wonderful, precious girl, wearing nothing but my wedding ring.'

She walked slowly towards him. 'Is that another of your plans—for the next hour or two?'

Nick lifted her into his arms and carried her to the bed. 'Make that a lifetime,' he whispered.

They lay holding each other and kissing. Savouring the brush and cling of each other's lips—the sensuous play of tongues. Until kissing became no longer enough.

Nick's hands were gentle as he began to unfasten the buttons on the turquoise dress. Cally arched towards him so that he could remove it completely, then, as he too began to undress, slipped swiftly and easily out of her underwear so that when he turned back to her she was waiting, just as he'd described.

Suddenly ridiculously self-conscious, she said, 'Adele told me I'm getting as big as a house.'

'Forget Adele, and her poison,' he commanded softly. 'And it's not true, anyway. You're only a very small cottage.'

He looked down at her lingeringly, his fingers drifting over her newly rounded nakedness with a kind of reverence.

'Oh, my darling,' he whispered unsteadily. 'Do you know how beautiful you are?'

She wasn't a beauty, and never had been, but she looked into his eyes and knew that was how he saw her. And that there were tears in the grey gaze adoring her with such tenderness.

It was as if every dream she had ever had was suddenly true, and with a small, inarticulate cry she pulled him down to her, reaching for him, her hand clasping him, guiding him between her thighs—then inside her, into the sweet molten core where he belonged.

Because she was so ready for him, and so very much more than willing.

Her body closed on him. Held him. Then moved with him slowly and softly in the first steps of love's dance. He treated her with infinite care, each powerful thrust of his body tempered with restraint. And she smiled against his mouth, making a few delicate adjustments, deliberately calculated to sabotage his self-control completely. Setting herself to wring every last atom of sensation from his strong male flesh.

Because she wanted him back, her passionate, skilful lover, who'd taught her all the enticements of desire during those long, fierce nights together. And she wanted him unguarded, vulnerable, and wholly hers—as, perhaps, he had never been before.

And at last, when both of them were driven beyond any limit they'd ever experienced together, she heard him sob her name as he spilled himself into her, and felt the glorious pulsations of her own release answering him.

Afterwards, she cradled him in her arms, his head pillowed on her breasts, his hand softly stroking her abdomen. And they murmured together—words of love, words of forgiveness and absolution.

There was a sudden note of laughter in her voice. 'I wonder what the baby made of that?'

'Probably thought it was being rocked to sleep,' Nick returned with a sigh of utter contentment.

'Mmm.' She was silent for a moment. 'Is it a relief to know you won't have to pretend any more—about Vanessa?'

'It has to be,' he admitted. 'There are some rough times ahead for her, and I want to be able to support her openly—although it will just be as a friend when her father's around.

My mother's right. He's one of the good guys. We shouldn't hurt him.'

'No.' She was quiet for a moment. 'Nick—why were you with her today? You never said.'

He said ruefully, 'She was altering her will, because the previous one left everything to Tony, and she asked me to be one of the witnesses. It wasn't an easy thing for her to do.'

'No,' she said, slowly. 'Poor Vanessa.' She hesitated. 'Do you think that she and I will become friends? I can't say she seemed to like me when we met.'

Nick propped himself up on an elbow, his face serious. 'Vanessa had to pick up the pieces after you left,' he said quietly. 'For a while there I was pretty much in self-destruct mode. So she sobered me up when I got drunk, and listened patiently when I tore myself in pieces over waking up next to some girl whose name I couldn't even remember.' He looked at her remorsefully. 'I'm not proud of that period in my life, darling. My only defence is that I was trying to blot you out for ever. But, however hard I tried, the pain of losing you just got worse.

'Vanessa was completely non-judgmental about it all—except once, when she told me frankly that it was unfair to take from women when I had nothing to offer in return. When I was simply using them because I couldn't have the girl I loved. She said if I was fool enough to want you that badly, then I should go and find you. Move heaven and earth to get you back, in spite of what you'd done.

'So it may take some time for her to come round. But she'll be mortified when she finds out what Adele really told you,' he added thoughtfully. 'And it will explain a lot, so that might help.'

'I'll just have to convince her that I'm here to stay.' Cally coaxed his head back to its former resting place, smoothing his dark hair from his forehead, then paused as she remembered something else. 'Nick—why do you want the Dower House back, if it's not for me? Was it just to get rid of Adele in case she made more trouble?'

'That was certainly an incentive,' he agreed. 'But I have another reason—one that I intended to discuss with you. My mother feels that life in a tent in some rainforest is fast losing its charm as she gets older. Becoming a grandmother has developed far more appeal for her, so she's considering a part-time post as a lecturer here in the UK. And she'd like to live in the Dower House—but only if you agree. She doesn't want to crowd us.'

She was smiling. 'I think it's a great idea. Our own built-in babysitter, no less. And perfectly used to dealing with a wilful small boy as well,' she added dreamily. 'How very useful.'

'Which is unfortunate,' Nick told her lazily, 'because we're having a sweet but stroppy girl.'

She shook her head. 'Boy first. Your son and heir.'

'A girl,' he said firmly. 'Or it's going back.'

'Ah, well,' she said. 'We won't argue the point. After all, you never know,' she added thoughtfully, 'it might be twins.'

And, one snowy January morning, that was exactly what it was...

If you enjoyed what you just read,
then we've got an offer you can't resist!

Take 2 bestselling
love stories FREE!
Plus get a FREE surprise gift!

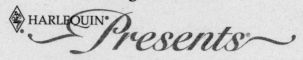

UNCUT

Even more passion for your reading pleasure...

Escape into a world of intense passion and scorching romance! You'll find the drama, the emotion, the international settings and happy endings that you've always loved in Harlequin Presents. But we've turned up the thermostat just a little, so that the relationships really sizzle.... Careful, they're almost too hot to handle!

VIRGIN FOR SALE
by Susan Stephens

#2515 January 2006

For one week ruthless billionaire Constantine Zagorakis will show businesswoman Lisa Bond the pleasure of being with a real man. But when the week is over they'll both pay a price they hadn't bargained on....

Presents

Will he get his wedding-night baby?

Virginal beauty Cally Maitland has become
accustomed to life on the run since fleeing her
marriage to British aristocrat Sir Nicholas Tempest.

But Nicholas isn't prepared to let Cally go. He has
a harsh ultimatum to deliver: give him their long-
overdue wedding night—and provide him with
an heir!

Legally wed, but he's
never said, "I love you."

HARLEQUIN®
Presents

Seduction and Passion Guaranteed

Harlequin Presents®
www.eHarlequin.com

ISBN 0-373-12509-7